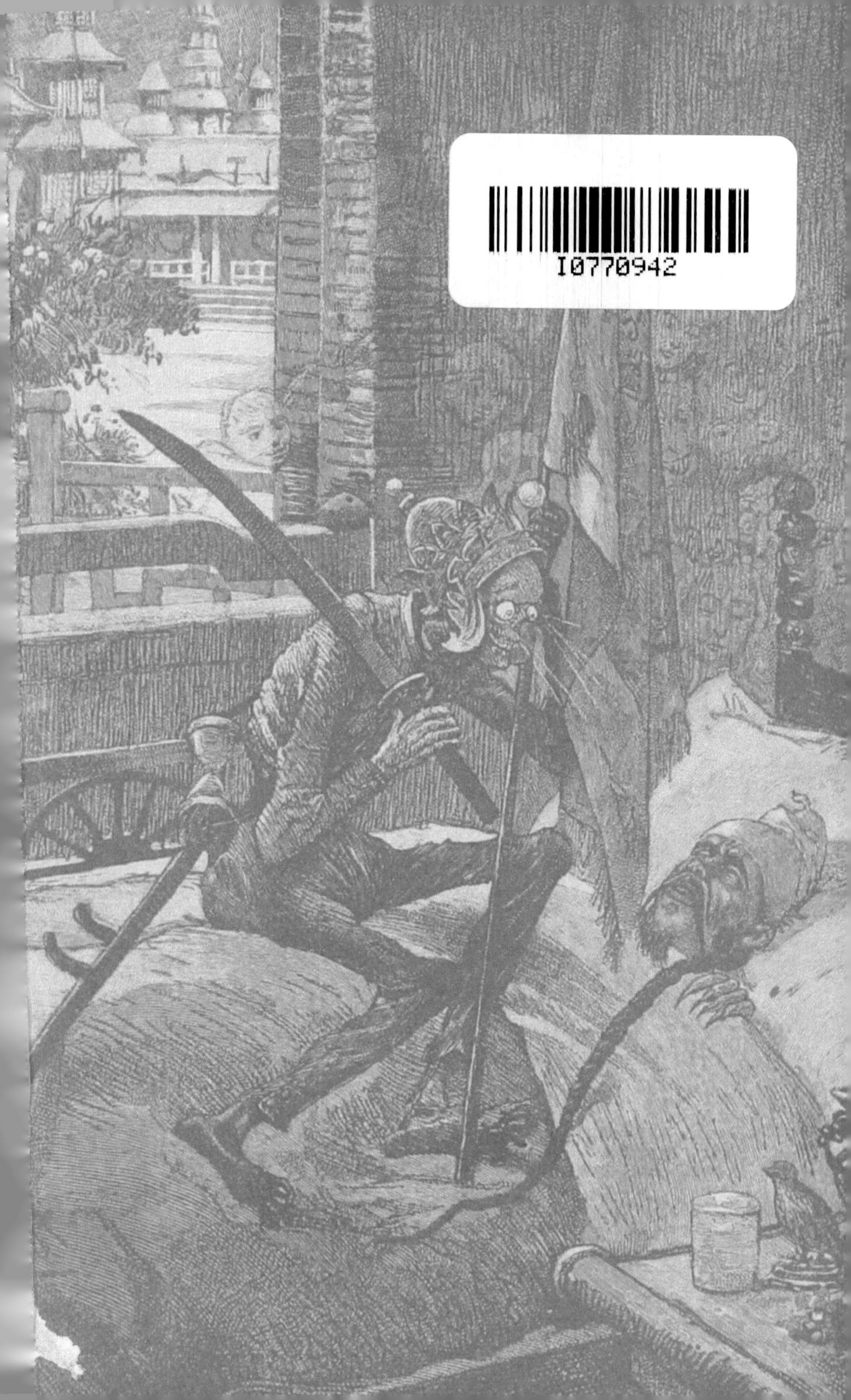

Madness Heart Press
2006 Idlewilde Run Dr.
Austin, Texas 78744

Copyright © 2025 John Baltisberger
Cover by Waclaw Traier
Edited by Lisa Lee Tone
Design by Nate Southard

First Edition
ISBN: 978-1-967517-09-1
www.MadnessHeartPress.com

Dying In the Dying
Lands

Table of Contents

Dying In the Dying Lands

A Note from John

The world of Mork Borg is dangerous, inspired by desperately heavy death metal and described as a "flail to the face in ttrpg form." Death is around every corner. The game really spawned an entire movement, and best of all, it seems like that movement is a sort of social disease. Third-party content creators just keep coming. Each new person who joins the community drags their friends along with them, just like I did for Kevin Welch, Nate Southard, and a smattering of others.

At the same time, the 3PP zeitgeist has spread to other games, games like Mothership, Obscure, and Primal actively encouraging their fans to roll up their sleeves and dig in. Of course, I would probably credit itch.io more for that particular movement than any other, but Mork Borg has such an insanely kind creator community. That brings us to this little collection of grim dark death.

Years ago, I offered a service, where if you sent me $15, I would write a piece of Kaiju flash fiction destroying the city of your choice. It didn't take off, but it was fun. While I was working on the Howling of the Unfortunate Dead Kickstarter, I was struggling to come up with some really fun ways to build out fun rewards, something that had a personal touch. That's when I came up with the idiotic idea of "Why don't I just write an entire second book just for the backers?"

Well here it is! This collection includes short stories of 17 of my friends, backers, and fellow Mork Borg creators being viciously murdered in the dying lands. Of course I couldn't stick just to the dying lands; I had to kill Brian Colin in his own Vast Grimm, and Zac Goins could only be taken out while sailing the Dark Caribbean of Pirate Borg.

Will there be a second collection? Probably. Eventually, I'll need to kill everyone in the community off, right? Only then will I be free to lift the 7th seal and unleash the final Misery that ends us all.

...

But in the meantime, enjoy these stories!

John Balisberger
The Mad Archivist

Jack of Hearts

(Kevin Welch)

"My name is Kevin Welch, and I ... am immortal." The bard grinned as he spoke to the small throng of peasants and commoners that gathered around. "I have been all around and throughout the lands from Kergus to Grift. I have explored Sarkesh and the svmp beyond! I have performed for Josilfa's choirs and danced for in the courts of Kage no Shima. I have faced a thousand deaths and lived one thousand and one lives."

Kevin reached up, stroking his long and wild beard, his eyes bright with the joy of the stories he could tell. "I have survived what no man can survive. Who would like to hear such a tale?"

There was a general murmur of interest. Kevin resisted the urge to roll his eyes—these fools wouldn't know quality entertainment if it crawled up their asses and died. It made his heart hurt. He shook off his irritation and smiled all the wider. "I mentioned I had performed in the courts of Kage no Shima, an island far to the east where demons encroach on the land. What I didn't say is that the customs of the isle are far different than those of our lovely Galgenbeck. There, it is honor that rules the land. All acts are done in single-minded servitude to this concept. It was there that a young knight—or a samurai, as they are called—attempted to save my honor by attempting to separate my head from my shoulders!"

Kevin lifted his beard, revealing a large discolored scar across this throat. There was another murmur in the crowd. He was gaining their interest, and in doing so, he would gain their coin.

"Or how about the time I was traveling across the ocean on a ship called *The Shackle*? A prison barge acting as a floating confinement for the very worst of the worst, men who were no longer men, women who embodied cruelty, and the undead crawling from every crevice in the ship. A vessel so inundated by evil as to warp the very nature of the sea around it. Would you like to know how I was able to escape? How I made it back to the mainland in one piece?"

"Bullshit!" a voice called, and a squalid tomato slammed into Kevin's chest, splattering him with its fetid juices. "You ain't got through all that. Ain't no one gonna survive that shit. You just lyin' to take our money." The man who was shouting at Kevin was toothless and filthy. It always was. The clean loved his stories. Those who had comfortable lives liked hearing about the danger far away from where they were. Con men and swindlers, on the other hand, hated him. There was nothing a manipulative bastard hated more than another manipulative bastard.

"Oh, is it? Is that what I am doing?" Kevin asked, a dangerous edge to his voice. "You are more than welcome to try to kill me if you think you can." Several people backed away, afraid of the sudden challenge, the sudden presence of danger there. "Of course, if you were to do that, you might discover that despite appearances, I am never alone. One does not *survive* in this world alone, no matter how immortal they may seem." He gestured to the crowd around him. "And who can say who is a bystander and who is a blade waiting in the crowd for anyone who might try to take my life?" He waited a few moments, his arms spread wide in invitation. When the man declined to strike, Kevin resumed his tales.

"Speaking of, my latest death defiance occurred only days ago. I was traveling with my companions, whomever they might be, as we delved deep into the ruined tower east of town. A wizard had hired us, you see, to recover a blade stolen from him. It was guarded, of course, by an assassin, who was after the blade, and by a horrid demon that guarded it. Now, I know what you are all thinking, that, somehow, I was poisoned or nearly ripped asunder. But the truth is that my near death was much more mundane!"

Kevin chuckled. "I was looting a body." He raised his hands to deflect the boos and gasps at his admission. "In these times, we need all the help we can get, and not only do the dead not need them, but it is better to deprive the undead of their weapons before they rise, right?" He watched people nod and agree before continuing. "So, I was looting a body when strange creatures flew up, blood red, trailing tendrils and limbs like a mosquito-hawk! One of the ghastly creatures slammed into my chest!" Kevin opened his tunic to reveal the red bruise across his ribs. "Here!"

The audience shrank back, and for a moment, Kevin was pleased that his story had the proper effect. A moment later, he realized it wasn't his story. His chest was aching terribly. Something cracked against his sternum from within, he could see the flesh of his chest distend and warp as a great mass of things underneath his flesh squirmed to be free.

"Wha ..." Kevin gasped, horror spreading across his face. But it was all he could manage to mutter before his ribcage exploded outward. Bone and gristle showered across the audience, their screams mingling with the screeches of the HeartBats that had hatched from the eggs laid in his chest just days ago. The small creatures swarmed through the throng of people, latching on any who were unfortunate enough to get in their way to feed and lay their own eggs.

Kevin's vision swam as he sank to his knees. His agony was complete, his immortality was over, but still, what a fucking story. He fell back into oblivion, a wide smile plastered across his dead face.

The Fratricide of Svoon

(Rollin Kunz)

Svoondrozh scratched his chin with his trunk. The elephantine Loxodon crouched on the craggy jetty above the Nameless Sea, watching the small waves break against the rocks, spraying him with beads of salty water. He had traveled the dying lands for too long, searching for something he truly did not wish to find. No, it was not desire that led him along his path but duty, an obligation that pulled him along the currents of life.

Here and now, he sought to fulfill that duty. Svoondrozh had followed the rumors of the many-legged monster across the coasts, all the way from Grift to this small seaside fishing village. He didn't know the name of the village, and no one would be able to tell him, not now. Their corpses littered the rocky outcroppings of the shoreline, broken, partially devoured. It was a gruesome sight but heartening nonetheless. The corpses were fresh. His quarry was close.

"Hello, Svoon." The voice called from behind him, making the Loxodon monster hunter stiffen. "I'm tired of running. Are you tired of chasing?"

Svoondrozh rose and turned, the bangles and charms that

dangled from his clothes jingling. He recognized the voice, though it was more ... gargled than he remembered. It was the voice of Devakumar, the creature he had been hunting for the better part of two decades.

"I only tire of finding your slaughter, monster." He spat the words at the Loxodon that had emerged from the village behind him. They looked *so* similar, but the other was haler, healthier looking, younger. A gift from his curse, Svoon was sure.

"Monster?" The other Loxodon chortled. "What a word to call your brother. And how many have you slaughtered? How many creatures have you sent to oblivion simply because they were too different in culture or morality? You are the butcher. I merely feed my hunger."

Svoon didn't care to listen to any more of his brother's shit. He trumpeted a challenge and charged towards his foe. Deva returned the trumpeted roar and surged to meet Svoon, but as he did, his body warped and changed, flesh stretching and bones dissolving to form monstrous tentacles that whipped forward to grab at Svoon.

Svoon grunted, bringing his arm up, the cestus he wore transforming into a buckler just in time to block Deva's mouth—now a terrifying beak surrounded by eight whipping tentacles and framed by two tusks—from slamming into him. He drew his arm back, the cestus reforming, then slammed the fist weapon into the hard beak.

The loud crack reverberated up his arm and shocked his shoulder, but the effect was more evident on Deva, as the octopus-Loxodon monstrosity fell back writhing. "You will finally be brought to justice," Svoon growled, walking forward, intent on strangling the life from his brother with his bare hands.

"Oh, will I?" Deva asked. He looked up with alien eyes, his tentacles lashing out and grabbing Svoon's ankles. Svoon was heavy, but Deva was terrifyingly strong. He pulled Svoon off his feet and spun, using momentum to pull Svoon off the ground, and hurled him through the sky.

Svoon landed in a heap on the rocky jetty, his hip screaming in agony. He was no longer a young warrior, and his own mass worked against him as he tried to rise. Deva approached, slowly shifting back into his natural Loxodon form. His face was a mass of bruises and broken bones and teeth, which healed even as Svoon watched.

"So this is it? You kill your brother and continue your massacre?" he said, reaching down into a pouch, searching for anything that might stave off death.

"This was your choice, Svoon. You could have stopped all this in Umberlee, you could have saved me from ever becoming this, and we both know you could have killed me shortly after ... You chose not to. You chose weakness. Every death I have ever caused is on your head. Including yours."

Deva rose to land the killing blow. At the same time, Svoon's hand closed around a vial in his bag, and without thought, he pulled the vial out and threw it with all of his might against Deva's chest. The glass exploded, showering them both with a fine red powder. Deva froze for a moment, his nose twitching.

"Paprika?" he finally asked. Svoon's eyes were wide as he realized he had grabbed the wrong vial. "At least you will taste delicious," Deva said as he fell upon Svoon, his body morphing back into a horrifyingly strange octopus. His beak found no resistance this time as it crashed into Svoon's skull and tore through the eye socket to take great gulping beakfuls of Svoon's cranial meat.

For an hour, the sounds of tearing meat and breaking bones floated across the near-empty beach, and then ... only the sound of the waves sung the eulogy of Svoondrozh, the Ingrown Nail of Umberlee.

War Never Changes

(Joseph Nahas)

This was war. It wasn't a good war, but in these fucked-up times, was anything good? For that matter, was war ever good? Joseph had thought so at one point. He had grown up reading about soldiers and mercenaries and the glory they attained. They had been heroes, cutting down villains and fucking princesses and all manner of amazing things that Joseph had long dreamed about. He had planned to leave home as soon as he was able to join the soldiers of some noble, or else sign on with a mercenary band to chase glory across the lands.

Then the Warhawk had come. He had ridden his white stallion in his gleaming armor right through Joseph's little town of Goitervurst looking for fresh recruits for his war effort. A war effort blessed by the Chvrch itself, a holy crusade into the Valley of the Unfortunate Dead to end the threat of the undead and maybe even waylay the apocalypse. This was it. This was better than signing on with a mercenary outfit! This was glory! This was destiny!

He had thrown down his rake and rushed to join, ignoring his father's stern admonishments and his mother's frightened wailing. They didn't understand. They didn't care about glory or honor. They weren't heroes. Not to him. The Warhawk had taken him and a handful of others from the town, given them weapons, armor, even training! After two weeks of grueling training with the sword, Joseph felt he could take on any challenge in the whole of the world.

He was wrong. The camp was being overrun.

All around him, the dead were swarming over the walls, and his arm was so damned tired. Joseph was bruised and hurt. He raised his sword to block the mace of a rotting skeleton, knocking it back and bringing his pommel down on the thing's skull. It was all he could do to push it back. His arms burned with exhaustion. The fight, a *real* fight, was taxing him to the very limits of his stamina. And there was no end in sight; the damned things just kept coming. He shifted his weight to his back foot, bringing his sword around to block another attack from the damned dead. There was no glory here. There were no heroes.

A lone trumpet sounded across the camp, and Joseph struggled to remember what the pattern of horn blasts meant. It took a few moments, the majority of his attention on not getting his skull caved in, but when he *did* remember, his heart nearly sang.

"Reinforcements!" he called, and turned his head to the east. There they were, a line of soldiers charging towards their location. At their head was Arik Bringare.

"Thank the Gods," Joseph whispered before remembering he could not waste time praying. He turned and threw himself at the monster that had been attacking him, his hope turning into fervor. He *could* survive this. He could become a hero like Arik!

He straddled the fallen skeleton and smashed down into its skull with his pommel again and again until the head was nothing but a fine bone powder, then rose and turned to face the soldiers coming again, a shout of joy on his lips. There was a man fighting next to Arik with a strange bladed buckler. It could only be Arik's brother, which meant there was not one but *two* slayers in the battle now! It was as good as won.

Joseph adjusted his grip on his sword. Now was the time. Now, he could show the slayers that he was skilled, that he had natural aptitude, that he could be one of *them*. He took a step forward to join them in their fray when he felt a bone hand on his shoulder. Before he could react, a blade punched through his chest. He looked down at the rusted and chipped weapon, marveling that something so ragged could cut so well. He couldn't feel his legs. He couldn't feel his arms. Everything was cold.

His mind went blank as darkness swallowed him. When he opened his eyes again, the world looked different. It was grainy and unreal, a swirling maelstrom of souls and pain. The sword was still in his chest, but that was a secondary concern. His main concern was protecting the Bone Heart, protecting his Lich masters. Joseph Nahas staggered forward, intent on ripping the living limb from limb.

The Last Catch
(Tommy Sunzenauer)

Sunze smiled up at the grey sky. The world was doomed. Misery after Misery unleashed. All things would die; all things would end. But none of this mattered to Sunze. The filthy alchemist pushed the pack off his shoulder and stretched. After two days of hiking, he was finally here. The small bubbling river flowed down from the springs located in the higher peaks, falling through the rocks in a cascading waterfall down to the flat section of the mountain he stood on now. The stream wrapped around the mountain from here, cutting a path through the rocks down to the valley below.

Sunze could hear the undead in the valley. Even as far below as they were, their moans carried on the wind up to him. But even that was not enough to dampen his spirits. For in this remote place, in this one locale far away from the cities and churches, Sunze was free. He pulled the flask from his hip and took a deep drink of the grain alcohol within. It burned its way down his throat, winding a path through his esophagus and gut that mirrored the stream.

The stream! That was why he was here.

Sunze belched and set the flask down as he pulled his

simple fishing gear from the pack. The dead were down in the valley, and there were no goblins or ghouls to bother him. The worst interruption he might face here was a stray goat harassing him for a snack. This was a good life. Sunze sat on a large rock next to the river and worked on fixing the line of his fishing rod, tying off the hook and finally affixing some bait. Everything was perfect now. Sunze looked up at the grey sky and considered saying an old fisherman's prayer but decided against it. If he couldn't see the sun, chances were the gods couldn't see him.

So instead of praying, Sunze took another swig from his flask and cast his line into the water. Once upon a time, he had had responsibilities and duties. Perhaps some people still thought he did. But the world was ending, and what was the point of earning coin when no one would live long enough to spend it? Better to just cast a line to catch dinner and while away the days in a haze of grain alcohol and trying to spot clouds that looked like naked women. A man had to have his hobbies.

Hours later, the sun was getting low over the mountains, and Sunze was well and truly pickled. He had had a few bites, but nothing substantial, nothing worth keeping and frying up. His stomach growled, and he felt the first vestiges of irritation poking through his drunken haze. Wouldn't it be just his luck? All the time in the world to fish, and some Misery comes along and steals all the fish. Just as he was postulating about the chances that Nechrubel was to blame for the lack of fish, something tugged on his line. Finally!

Sunze rose with an excited yelp and pulled his rod back. Whatever was on the other end of his line was big, bigger than he would have expected from the stream. He didn't question it; he just wrestled with it. He worked the rod back and forth, countering the movements of the growing shadow in the water. Sunze grit his teeth and pulled hard, wrenching the big fucker out of the water onto the shore, where it twitched and flopped about.

It was a beautiful salmon, fat and healthy, its scales shining in the dull light as it gasped and spasmed across the muddy shore of the stream. "Haha!" Sunze screeched and leapt forward, reaching to his belt to pull free the cleaver he kept there. He set a foot on the body of the fish and swung down, decapitating the thing in a mighty display of near perfect fish butchery.

Sunze's self-satisfaction was short-lived, however. Something black poured from the fish's wound. A blanket of twitching legs and tiny black bodies. Long-legged spiders flooded out of the piscine corpse in impossible numbers. Sunze's blood ran cold, and he took several steps backward as he watched the mass of arachnids subsume the fish entirely. But they just kept coming, the pile of spiders becoming a mound and then spilling down. A black, inky pool of jittering movement that just kept spreading.

Sunze stared in horrified shock until he felt movement on his leg, something touching him. He glanced down. The black pool had reached him, a tendril of bouncing spiders swarming over his foot and touching his leg. That was too much for Sunze. He let out a terrified bellow and turned on his heel to run. He was already three steps ahead before his short-circuiting brain remembered where he was. He tried to stop, but the loose gravely rocks under his feet would not give him traction, and he tumbled forward and over the side of the cliff.

He tumbled through the air and tried to scream as a torrent of spiders followed him over the edge of the cliff, millions of the creatures tumbling down after him. How? How did they fall faster than him? The creatures reached him, scrambling onto his plummeting body, finding their way into his mouth, his nose, his ears.

Sunze pushed a spider out of his mouth with his tongue and tried to scream a prayer. The sudden impact with the earth below cut him off as it pulverized his lungs and powdered his bones. His brain survived only long enough to witness the torrential rain of tiny spiders descending over him. His world was blanketed in black, twitching bodies, and in the distance, like the rolling of thunder, Nechrubel laughed.

An Education

(Matthew Henshaw)

"**Y**ou stand accused of heresy, Herr Henshaw, how do you plead?"

"Innocent! Of course, I'm innocent. I'm no heretic; I'm a school teacher!" Mattias Henshaw said. He narrowed his eyes, trying to make out his accuser, but they had stripped him of his glasses, leaving him nearly blind.

"A teacher!" the Inquisitor cried, appealing to the audience of priests sitting in attendance. "What better position for a man dedicated to plying our youth with lies and heresies? What better place than in a schoolhouse to whisper your insidious mockeries to the holy church in the ears of the impressionable?"

"No!" Mattias shouted. "By HE and SHE, no. I'm no such monster; I swear on the graves of my parents. I merely teach reading and writing. Reading that they may read the scriptures of the church, writing so they may spread it. These are holy endeavors. I am of one mind with you. I am a loyal servant of—"

"Silence, Herr Henshaw!" the mad priest cut him off. "Still your lying tongue lest I am forced to remove it. And if

I *did* remove your tongue, how then would you confess your sins and repent of them?" The priest came close, his blurry outline filling Mattias's view. He struggled against his bonds but to no avail. He was strapped to a large wood slab, tilted at an angle so that he was easily visible to the viewing gallery.

"Please," he sobbed. "I don't even know how I could have possibly been accused. I have no enemies. I have supported my students, my friends. I have no great wealth to spark jealousy, no power to create outrage, just my wife, my job, and my life."

"And now all three are lost," snapped the priest. "Your school is closed, your wife accused of foul witchery, and your life ... your life is over, Herr Henshaw. You may only choose if your life is over quickly with confession willingly on your lips, or whether I will be forced to pull it from you slowly. I suggest the latter." The blurry shape swept its arm as though indicating something else in the murky room. "My fellow priests, here to witness the good work, they do so enjoy a show."

"My wife," Mattias whimpered. "She is innocent. She's no witch. She's the kindest soul there is."

"You say the same thing about yourself, Henshaw. It doesn't matter; we'll pull the truth from you along with your intestines." The Inquisitor laughed cruelly and reached for something out of Mattias's field of vision. When he lifted his hand, he held a long sliver of shining metal. Mattias could only assume it was a knife.

"No. No. Not my wife! You leave her alone! You don't touch her!" Mattias struggled against his bindings, more concerned with the news his wife might be taken than he was with his personal safety. But that had always been his way. He had always fought hard to protect and care for others more than himself.

"Leave her alone? Touch her?" scoffed the priest. "My

dear Henshaw, she was burned at the stake this morning. Her confession to heresy and witchcraft was not easy to dredge up, but she *did* confess in the end. And so will you."

Mattias felt the blade at his sternum. It was sharp, and he could feel the sting as it slipped through his skin and parted flesh, muscle, and fat almost effortlessly. He did not pull away. He did not struggle. The news of his poor wife's demise was a more painful torture than anything anyone could do to him. He spoke calmly, his voice dead and cold. "Then pull out what you will. May the black toad devour your souls and hold them in the depths of the infernal swamp for all eternity."

"So you confess?" The Inquisitor sounded almost sad. He dug his hand into Mattias's guts, looping a hand around a fold of his intestines and quickly pulling it through the incision he'd made. He was eager to enact some of the cruelty in his heart and would not be spoiled of his fun by Mattias giving in too quickly.

"I confess only to murder!" Henshaw spat. "Namely, yours."

The intestines in the Inquisitor's hand writhed, suddenly too alive. It coiled around the priest like a serpent, lifting him from the floor and smashing him into the wall. The room was filled with screams as two webbed hands, larger than could possibly exist inside the man, thrust out of the hole in Henshaw. They were followed by spindly arms and then the great head of a horrible black toad. As soon as its mouth was free, it opened wide. A tongue covered in corrosive slime and bony spikes shot out. It crushed one of the priests' heads and drew the victim in, already dissolving him alive, then swallowed the man whole.

More intestinal tendrils, revealed to be part of the toad-thing, lashed out. They flung fecal digestive juices around the room. Where the fluid landed, smaller black toads emerged, smaller clones of the massive monster clawing its way into reality from Henshaw's ruined torso.

The priests struggled to fight their way to the door, but their panicked fingers were clumsy; their flesh, dissolving, slipping from their bones like aged rags. The small toads were swelling, filling the room, their appetite for flesh growing with them. Finally, the door was open. A priest made it two steps into the hallway before a spiked tongue smashed through his ribcage from behind and pulled him back in.

But now the toads were free of the room. They spilled out into the church fortress, a plague of spawning amphibious death. Over the noise of croaking death and human screams, Henshaw, dead and damned, laughed with abandon.

Rotten Fruit

(Harlen Linke)

"Rum da da dum da dum da dum dum." Harlen whispered the sounds out as he put the produce out onto the stand. Market days were his least favorite days. While it was easier work selling fruits from lord's little farm and orchard than it was to actually grow it, he still hated it. It meant that instead of being on his own for the day, minding his own business and coming up with fun songs to play with his friends, he would be forced to interact with people. Gross.

The day was long, and the sales were piss-poor. The crops had been beyond lackluster. The apples were shriveled little things, bitter to taste and mealy in texture. The cabbage was good, but everyone was tired of cabbage. Cabbage wrapped around mealy fruit for breakfast, steamed cabbage for lunch, boiled cabbage and anemic chicken for dinner. But still, Harlen tried, calling to those passing by to see if they would partake of his wares. He just needed to sell enough to make his wages. The lord was fond of telling him that he was only worth what he made, and if he ever made less than he was worth, well, then maybe he would be worth more as mincemeat for the lord's hounds.

It wasn't looking good.

At the rate it was going, Harlen figured he might as well start making plans for what sort of gravy should go with his flesh for the dogs. Each rush through the market made him hopeful, and each time it thinned out, the reality of his piss-poor sales came crashing down around him. He didn't know for sure that his lord would *actually* kill him and feed him to his pets, but he didn't *not* know that either. By the time the sky began to darken, Harlen was considering where he might disappear to. He could always just ... go, elope into the wilderness and start a new life in a new town. Maybe Grift? He heard they liked to party there. He could probably get a gig as a musician for some lord or lady who liked throwing weird end-of-days galas. He closed his eyes, picturing what that sort of life might be like.

"Cabbage?!" The voice was something between a shriek and a bellow, a discordant rasp that somehow hit two notes at the same time. The sound felt like an attack, and it was so sudden that it actually made Harlen recoil for a moment as he opened his eyes. Standing in front of him was a disheveled old man. He wore green and brown robes—or at least Harlen thought they were green and brown; it could have just been all the muck stuck to them. Various mushrooms grew off of the man, and he stank of mildew and ...

Harlen knew that other smell. The skunky stink of the medicinal herb. It immediately brought his anxiety down, made the strange figure before him more comforting, and made Harlen wish he could go home right now and partake of the herb himself. The swamp-man stared at him with wild, bloodshot eyes.

"Huh?" Harlen finally responded to the question.

"CABBAGES?!" the man scream-bellowed again.

Harlen looked around the market. A few people were staring, but mostly, people seemed to be trying to ignore whatever was happening at his booth. "Uh ... yes ... sir," Harlen said. "And apples," he finished helpfully.

"Cabbages," the man repeated, lifting one and turning it in his hand as though he were pondering the leafy orb for its secrets. It occurred to Harlen that the man might be some sort of wizard; he was certainly unclean enough. He looked and smelled as though he made his home in a swamp or marsh. And one never knew what sort of eccentrics a spell-caster might get into. The magic, as Harlen understood it, boiled your brain faster that the herb.

"Three cabbages!" the bog wizard snarled and slapped three bent and dirty coins on the counter of the stall.

"Oh, yes, m'lord!" Harlen said quickly, finding his two best cabbages and presenting them to the man.

He inspected them the same way he had the first and nodded. "And what else?"

"Oh ... well, I have apples?" Harlen muttered and set one of the mealy fruits in front of the wizard. The wizard lifted one, the skin buckling under even the lightest of pressure. Harlen winced as the wizard's face crumpled into a disgusted expression.

"You call these apples? Apples!" the bog wizard shouted at him. "I'll give you apples!"

"No, sir, I just meant that—" Harlen began.

"Appledash! Applecrash! Apples of death and doom!" the wizard screamed, flecks of phlegm and spit showering Harlen's face. He pointed a long and gnarled finger at Harlen and hissed in a terrifying language that sounded like it would sit more comfortably on the tongues of toads rather than in a human mouth. "THEN BE THE APPLE!" the wizard finished.

A pale yellow-green light formed around the wizard's hands, a viscous illumination that dripped and oozed across his flesh before it launched itself at Harlen and enveloped his head. It was damp and cold, with a texture like moist snot as it invaded his nostrils and mouth. Harlen's screams were cut off by the mucus-light as it pushed past his teeth and down his throat.

Everywhere the light touched was transformed. His flesh became more porous, slimy. He was shrinking too, becoming smaller and smaller, his flesh turning from pink to green and covered in little warts and growths. He wanted to shout, to beg for release, but all that came out was an echoing croak. Harlen's eyes bulged out of his skull, his lips widening until they nearly split his head in half, but still he shrank until he had to use his strange amphibian hands to crawl out from the pile of his clothes. Harlen slowly blinked, his throat sack expanding as he croaked in protest at his new form.

"That's what you get!" the wizard shouted. "Lord of apples no more, I name you frog lord." The bog wizard laughed again before lifting his leg and bringing his heel down onto the Harlen-frog, easily crushing the life out of him and splattering his intestines all across the cobblestone walk of the market grounds. No one dared move or protest as the bog wizard lifted his cabbages from the counter, scraped his boot off on a nearby stone, and made his way back towards his swampy abode.

Rime of the Salty Mariner

(Zac Goins)

They were singing again.

Goddamn them, always with the singing. Master Zacharius Goins had enjoyed the singing at first. The call and response filled the long hours and made the work seem more of a dance, a complex choreography of movement that kept the ship going through all hours. But after a lifetime of service to the ships of the Dark Caribbean and thirty years wed to the sea, Master Goins was ready for an annulment.

"Haul on the bowline indeed," Zac grumbled as he moved through the ship. He had spent the better part of four decades of life on board ships and could remain upright during the fiercest storm. Once upon a time, this life had been exciting. He had woken each day to the majesty of the sea, the camaraderie of the crew, and the absolute danger of a life of piracy. Now, as the grizzled quartermaster of the *Victoria's Hatred,* Zac rarely bothered getting to know the crew beyond their names and their earnings. Truly, if he knew someone better than that, it was due to their pay being docked enough times to become a nuisance. The majority of these salty men would be lost to the sea or, worse, to the ash.

Zac paused at the mess, checking in on the rations and stores on the ship. Soon, they would need to make landfall and restock, likely raid a settlement for food, maybe hold it for ransom if they could hold it.

"Ship ho!" The call came from the deck.

Zac cursed under his breath as he lumbered through the tight hallways of the vessel to join the crew topside. Everyone was gathered to portside, trying to make out the colors of the vessel just visible on the horizon. Normally, whoever was taking a shift in the crow's nest would have called it out. Their silence could only mean they didn't have the first clue as to who was approaching.

"Worthless green-gills." Zac sighed before pulling his collapsible eye-piece out of his vest and bringing it to his eye. It took him a few seconds to find the ship. When he did, he felt the blood drain from his face. He knew that flag, and he understood why the lookout had not. No one who hadn't personally faced down the Lord Inquisitor's personal vessel would know it, and there were too few of those who lived to tell the tale. "Hoist the sails, damn ye! Catch the wind and make swift!" Zac stomped away from the railing and moved to lend his own practiced strength to pulling the main sails into place.

"What is it, Master Goins?" one sailor asked as he set about the work alongside the Quartermaster.

"The very devil," Zac spat. "Oi, you lot!" he called over his shoulder to some men milling about. "Get you te the cannons! Prepare full broadsides!"

"Master Goins, what in Basatan's clacking claws are ye goin' on about? Yer shoutin' orders awful free."

Zac looked up from his work into the one good eye of Captain Geoffrey Dennis and nearly snarled his answer. "Tis the *Purity o' Purpose,* Cap'n. That be the ship o' Sotomayor."

It took Captain Dennis a few moments to connect the

ship's name and captain in his mind, but as it clicked, he began to roar orders as well. They were pirates and heretics, faithful servants of coin first and foremost and followers of Basatan after that. They would all hang from the noose at best should the Inquisition catch them.

"No worries, Master Goins!" The young sailor that had helped him with the sales chuckled. "We're far ahead o'em. We'll be a memory of foam and salt before they can get close enough to make us."

"Shut yer trap, boy," Zac growled as he moved away from the rope to watch the oncoming Inquisition ship. The boy didn't know. He hadn't been out here long enough to witness what Zac had; he didn't know what Zac knew.

"Doldrums!" someone shouted needlessly.

Indeed, the sails took still, as though there were not a breeze in the world that could fill the canvas and propel them. Normally, in any conditions, Zac would put his doubloons on their frigate outrunning any ship the navy or the Inquisition could throw at them. These were not normal conditions. He pulled his eyepiece out and looked towards their enemy. Their sails were billowing, full of wind, as though Poseidon himself was at their back blowing air to drive the damned ship forward. Around them, rain began to pour down upon them, thunder cracking the sky.

"Sorcery," Zac spat, then raised his voice to shout over the noise of the crew. "We'll have to fight. Prepare te be boarded, lads. Draw your blades, prime yer pistols, prepare te welcome Lord Sotomayor." Zac knew it was a hopeless fight. He had—a lifetime ago—sailed on the *Purity*. He knew exactly what sort of monster was running them down. He could almost hear him now, the stench of ash-tainted tobacco cloying in the Spaniard's beard as he hoarsely spoke.

"Hola, Maestre Goins."

Zac spun where he stood, his sword out of its sheath in a

breath and slashing through the air where the ghostly image of High Inquisitor Antonio de Sotomayor stood. "Damn ye," Zac growled, his free hand raising to clutch the pendant of Basatan that hung around his neck.

"Damn me?" The apparition laughed. "You have damned yourself, pandejo. Worshipping gods of the depths. You disappoint me."

"Come here to my face and speak it. You'll find we are a difficult lot to take back for your little tortures and executions." Zac growled.

"Oh ... you think ..." Sotomayor grinned wide. "No worries there. I have no intention of bringing any of you back alive. You are not worth the time." The image of the Inquisitor glanced to the side and nodded. "Fire when ready." He turned his ghostly eyes back to Zac. "Adios, Maestre Goins. You go to serve your damned god."

Zac roared and swept his sword uselessly through the fading image of his hated former employer. It was as worthless and ineffectual as his leather armor was against the onrushing grapeshot that tore through him, leaving a fine red mist where the man used to stand. Giblets of Goins scattered across the ocean, bits of meat and organs unmoored from their bodily prison and left to sink into the darkness of Davy Jones' locker.

Would Zac be elated to know that the clacking claws of the crustacean god's children pulled the bits that floated down to devour? Or would his soul be too busy screaming in the agony of being ripped asunder for all eternity by the hungry deep god? Only Basatan knows.

Bad Trip

(Bridget Brave)

Bridget the Brave. What a moniker. Bridget always appreciated the title, what it meant, what it said about them to the various fuckwits and peasantry. But more than those unfortunate souls, they liked what it said about them to the nobles and merchants who were looking to spend their coin on protection ... or a hired killer.

Bridget was both. They had honed their skills across what felt like hundreds of jobs and honed their blade across what was certainly dozens of throats. It was a good life. But at the same time, Bridget wished they could abandon it along with the title. Being the go-to merc for dangerous and daunting jobs paid well. But it was harrowing, and all they really wanted to do was sit in their manor, smoking those herbs that allowed their mind to drift into oblivion while surrounded by cats. *That* was their goal.

But instead of lazily watching a fire burn surrounded by cats and the thick, acrid smoke of higher consciousness, they were in a ruined fort, blade in hand, hunting down a mongrel waste of a man who had thought he could get away with fucking a duke's wife. Imagine the balls on that man! To sleep with a duke's wife was pretty much asking to be hunted down. Not that the duke wasn't an adulterous piece of shit too. They all were, but to let yourself get caught? That was entirely different.

Bridget sneaked through the shadows of the fort, as silent as the dust that floated along the dim shafts of greyish light coming in through the holes in the ceiling above.

These were their stomping grounds. Ruins, caves, and desolate places where the long arm of justice might be eluded. But it couldn't. Too many desperate men and women eager to accept blood-soaked coin in exchange for atrocities meted out in proxy for the rich and powerful. And what was the use? How many Miseries had come and gone? How close was the world to truly ending? Doing things for coins that would soon be as meaningless as the morality that the world had left behind long ago seemed a certain kind of madness.

This would be Bridget's last job, her last foray into the dark places for a handful of silver. They was resolute. They would spend the rest of the world's days with the cats and weeds that made living and dying bearable.

These were the thoughts that filled Bridget's head as they crept through the third story of the ruins. Their blade had sung its song through a handful of their prey's vassals. The screams would have alerted the man they hunted. He would be ready for them. Not that it mattered. Ready or not, whether he fought, begged, or surrendered, the result would be the same. They would cut out his tongue and his eye and return them to the duke, and then ... then peace.

There! Ahead, they saw the silhouette of a man. He stood next to what had once been a window, now a shattered hole in the wall of the crumbling fort. His arms hung limply by his sides, no weapon in sight. In their youth, Bridget would have been annoyed by the lack of a challenge, the absence of a good fight. Now, they didn't care. They didn't do it for the thrill. They approached, abandoning the shadows altogether as they came closer to their quarry.

"I see you," the man said.

"I know," Bridget responded as they walked forward.

"I heard them. Are they all …?"

"Every last one," they answered.

"Why? Because I loved a woman? Because I dared to give her the affection her husband wouldn't?" he asked.

Bridget was sickened by the sight of the man. He trembled and hung his head. He was trying to be indignant, to be angry. But he had soiled himself, the piss pooling at his feet, giving lie to any projected bravery he might pretend at.

"You loved her?" Bridget asked, putting a worm of care in their voice.

"I did," he answered, jutting out his chin in defiance.

"And she loved you?" Bridget pressed, coming to a stop a foot or so away from the target of their current task.

"She did," he said, seeming to take strength from the statement—well, as much strength as one could have when standing in a puddle of their own urine.

"Then you should return to her. You should run to her, be with her," Bridget said, their voice full of conviction. "The world is ending. Darkness is everywhere. Love, love is the only thing that should matter. Go to her," they pressed.

"You would let me?" he asked softly.

"Yes."

"I don't even know how. How can I reach her now?" he asked, turning away from her to stare over the horizon, his breathing slowing.

"Don't worry," Bridget said softly. "I know a shortcut."

They leaned back, lifted their leg, and kicked the man in the middle of the back, sending him flying through the window. He screamed as he fell, a scream cut short by a wet slap. Bridget wondered if he understood what was happening.

The duchess had already been put to death. If he wanted to be with her, he could do so in hell. If hell existed. Bridget leaned over to see the fruit of their labor. There he was, sprawled on the cobblestones below in a rapidly spreading pool of blood, limbs at odd angles. But mostly intact—they could still fetch the hand and eye.

Bridget turned on their heel, intent on making their way downstairs, but lost their traction on the urine-slick stone and slipped. Their arms wheeled as they tried and failed to catch their balance. They screamed a curse and fell back, out of the hole in the wall. It was not a scream of fear, but of rage and frustration. Their last thought as they plummeted to their death was not one of regret but rather how perhaps this was best. Perhaps they were just taking a shortcut to the end, skipping the line of misery and waiting.

Then Bridget thought no more, their brains scattered across the stones, just more meat for the wolves.

Wrongful

(Christian Eichhorn)

C hristian Eichhorn sat in the bar watching the other patrons with barely disguised loathing. Another night of drunkards and whores engaging in the dance of debauchery and tedium that Christian had long grown bored of. He had no taste for it any longer. Not that he judged those who lived in their cups or those who sold their bodies for coin while trading disease far and wide. He had partaken of both excesses enough times in his own squalid youth. Rather, he judged them for their lack of creativity. These so-called men who drank as though drink were the grandest thing. These women who would lay on their backs to take a rutting before pouring a glass of water over themselves to hide the stench of the last for the next.

Didn't they know there were far more interesting compounds and substances to enjoy than mead and ale? Things that would turn their minds inside and out and show them the faces of dead gods who would whisper deader secrets into their ears? And the whores. Gods, the whores. He could show them such excitement, such positions and toys and acts that would debase the very earth they stood on. If you were to hire a woman whose concept of decency was dead, why pretend at it? With enough coin, they could rut in a way that would make the very devils sit up and take notice.

But that was all past. He had tried for a while to spread his gospel of excess to the masses in Grift. Meeting in clandestine gatherings where he would share narcotic bliss and sexual perversion, encouraging not only consumption but participation and innovation as well. Time and time again, just as he was beginning to feel as though he was converting new followers to his ways, things would end. Either his students would become burnt out and retreat from the face of greatness or else would slip too deeply beyond the binds of what a human body was capable of. At least those that had died did so in great bacchanals of debased pleasure, limbs and flesh stretched on hooks while out of their minds on arcane powders that left their brains and souls dribbling out of their orifices. It was a good death. Better than the deaths that he had escaped every time the Inquisition caught up to him.

Now ... now even he was tired. He was bored. He was defeated. Why gather together those eager students if they would just surrender to mundanity? Why push for new experience if that new experience couldn't lead to greater acts? No, he would simply wallow in his anger and self-pity, drown his sorrow and boredom in the glasses of piss-water that the locals called beer, waiting for the world to die as it deserved to.

"Kristibel Echton?"

The name almost slipped across Christian's mind without registering. Why would it? It was not his name. It wasn't even one of the many aliases he had used over the years while dealing in his horrid craft of flesh exploration.

"It is you, ain't it?" the man said, spitting the accusation at him with barely contained hatred.

"No, sir, my name is Eichhorn," Christian said softly, trying to seem small and unassuming. "You have the wrong man."

"No, no, I don't," the man said, pulling a knife. "Kristibel owes my boss, Mister Kicman, more than a spit of silver, and he says to me, 'Fetch the silver from that no good Echton or fetch me his tongue.' So, Mister Echton, which will I be fetching today?"

Christian frowned at the sight of the blade. He wasn't afraid of it, not at all. His hand slipped inside his cloak, where he kept the sharp flensing knife—as useful in pleasure as it was in pain—his fingers wrapping around the ornate hilt shaped like a woman pleasuring herself. "I said you have the wrong man," he said firmly.

"And I says I don't," the man growled.

Christian did not wait for the situation to grow more tense. His hand lashed out, drawing a bright red line from ear to ear across the man's throat. The man's eyes went wide as he tried to process what had just happened. Christian watched calmly as the wound opened up and poured the man's life across the table. He felt nothing as he watched the man die, flopping about on the table and then the floor like a gutted fish. Calmly, he rose and stepped around the body, ready to make his escape and find a new hellhole to await the end.

Perhaps he had grown too lazy; perhaps he was too confident. Whatever the reason, he did not notice the other shadow sweep across the table, not until something heavy and hard slammed into his chest, slipping between the ribs to kiss his heart.

"Master Kicman sends his regards," the lout whispered in his ear, his scratchy beard rubbing Eichhorn's face as he fell back, his eyes locked onto the hilt of the blade protruding from his chest.

This? This was how he died? Stabbed by a common thug

n a pub? Such a lazy death. He had tasted so many excesses,
o many outlandish acts of hedonistic savagery; never did he
hink that his life would be ended so basely. He had expected
is death to be explosive, but now, he watched as all the world
imply ... faded ... away.

Wah

(Charles Bernard)

The circus was in town!

Galgenbeck was alive with excitement. The red and gold tents of the traveling show had sprung up seemingly overnight. There was a petting zoo filled with strange looking animals, a freak-a-torium with all manner of disturbing survivors of arcane and scientific exploration, a fortune teller that claimed to be sanctioned by the Chvrch, and so much more.

But the main attraction was the show. A multihued tent where the ringmaster, one Master Teeth, would bark out the eccentricities of the performers for all to see. For a meager two coins, any man, woman, or child could find their seat and watch the greatest show in the world.

And what a show it was! Here were the juggler brothers, four identical quadruplets tossing blades and flaming torches between them, the painted smiles on their faces hiding the myriad of scars. Over in this ring, an old man with a whip and a wooden chair directed fierce wild animals to leap through rings of fire. There were trapeze artists and contortionists, dazzling displays of acrobatics and sword swallowing. But what everyone wanted was the clowns!

Ah, the clowns. There were so many, like a rainbow had vomited living people out into the tent. They swarmed the stands and rings with their slapstick humor and mimed acts of violence. The tent was filled with laughter, and then the lights dimmed, the spotlight shuttered to direct all attention on the center ring. Master Teeth stood tall and proud in his garish purple finery, his smile so wide as to be unnerving, but it was easily seen from the farthest seats in the house.

"My friends!" he called through the cone of his speaking horn, amplifying his voice to the whole of the audience. "We have seen spectacle beyond spectacle. We have seen the death-defying acts of bravery, of skill, of sheer determination! But I know what you have come for, what you have *truly* come for. The one and only mage-clown in all of the lands."

It was so quiet you could hear a pin drop. He was right; the clown with a wizard's training was all anyone could talk about in the week leading up to the show. Rumors permeated society in how such a man could accrue such power and then abuse such power so casually. It was a mystery worth exploring.

Some said he was a disgraced court mage whose power had waned and had been forced to instead pick up the jester's wand. Some postulated that he was an adventurer who had stumbled across unclean scrolls of power and been driven mad by their secret and profane knowledge. And yet a few muttered in the shadows that he was always a clown but one whom had ascended from hell's courts, an infernal jester sent to make the world laugh through the end of reality.

All present wanted to know the truth. All present feared what the truth would reveal.

With the booming sound of arcane trumpets, the lights went out. A scream rent the darkness, and just as suddenly as they had been plunged into the darkness, a single light lit on the center ring. There he stood. Smashy the Arcane Jester. Clown and mage extraordinaire. Smashy's grease paint face was stretched into a ferocious grin as he danced across the ring. He spread his hands, and fireworks sprouted from his palms, launching up and booming in an explosion of light, drawing gasps of delight from children.

He cartwheeled across the dirt, producing a massive hammer from nothing and slamming it down. Where he slammed the hammer down, homunculi of dirt and mud rose. A dozen or more of the dirt simulacrum staggered towards Smashy as he continued his inane act. But with a snap of his fingers, Smashy summoned strange pies that he then threw with all of his might at the creatures.

With each impact, they dissolved, the creme mixing with the dirt and melting the things as though it was acid and not custard that hit the shambling monsters. The audience hooted and hollered, delighted and terrified at the spectacle of magic so freely used. When all the creatures had returned to the earth, Smashy paused, taking long, ridiculously foppish steps across the ring, studiously avoiding the spent pie tins. He turned to face the audience and held up a finger, enticing them to wait and see what was next.

Smashy rolled up his sleeves, revealing arms heavily tattooed with arcane sigils, and lifted his hands high. Power rolled across his palms, arcane light tracing his digits. The light cast his clownish visage in a malignant hue, and all held their breath. Then it sputtered out. There was a wave of quiet laughter at the clown's antics, but Smashy did not look amused.

His painted smile twitched, almost becoming serene as his actual lips turned down in a frown, and then he screamed. It was the first sound he had made with his own voice in decades, a raw, bloody thing that was wrenched out of him by intense unspeakable agony. His arm deflated, bulging abnormally as his fingers, then wrist went limp, as though he was a scarecrow losing his straw. All eyes watched him as he took a clumsy step forward and fell to his knees. No one helped.

His other arm began to bulge and writhe, following suit with the first, and the two boneless limbs hung uselessly as his sides. There were those in the audience who understood what was happening, but they did not move to help. They knew this was simply the price of being cavalier with magic. It was no toy, no plaything, and it would exact a price in flesh. Flesh *and* bone.

Skeletal hands thrust through the flesh of Smashy's face, ripping and tearing the meat away from the bone, and Smashy's skeleton pulled its way free of its skin-prison. It raised its bony grin to the heavens and clattered a hollow war cry as it shed the remains of the clown, now no more than any of the dirt golems he had created earlier. There were cries and warnings; men drew swords. But the bones of Smashy was having none of it. With a curtsy and a bow, the bones turned and dashed out of the spotlight and into the dark mire of the circus, trailing entrails and shedding organs as it did.

By the time the lights came on, there was no sign of the clown's innards, only the soft pliable leather of his outward appearance resting in the bloody dirt.

Divine Beast

(Simone Tammetta)

The forests of Sarkesh were damned. This was not the superstitions of Simone's tribe; this was fact. The only things living here were twisted creatures, warped by the unnatural energies that permeated the foliage. Most of the tribes and nearly all of the civilized men of these scattered kingdoms were fearful of the shadows and monsters that resided within the forest. But not Simone of the Tammetta. He had grown grey in the shadows of these trees, etching out a life in those cursed lands for himself and his tribesmen. It was a hard life, but this did not matter; he was a hard man.

But he was old and broken.

He had fought too many battles.

He had taken too many heads.

He was just too gods-damned tired.

Let the civilized world worry about the Basilisks and their prophecies. Let the nonces in their castles care of cults and the soul. Simone was no weak-willed thing with water in his veins. He would die, yes, but he would choose his death, and he had chosen a good one.

Simone stalked between the trees. The axe on his shoulder

was nearly as old as he was. He had carried it for forty years now, though the handle had been replaced, the head honed time and again. It would be custom to pass the weapon down to his child. But his children were dead. His grandchildren too. All that was left was him, and soon, he would pass through the miasma of life to emerge on the eternal battlefields of Hel. He would take his rage with him to the demons and devils there, crush their life out of their bodies with his bare fists. They would answer for his pain. They would pay.

Simone paused in his ruminations. What was that? He turned his head slowly, inhaling the stale stench of the forest, tasting the air. He could smell the rancid odor of rot. The sort of stink that came from meat trapped on teeth, marinating in the saliva of some awful creature.

It was hunting him.

Simone's grey beard parted as he smiled. No, it *thought* it was hunting him. He rolled his neck and shoulders, loosening his aching muscles. The beast saw an aged human, lost and alone in Sarkesh. Beasts had no concept of honor, no ideas toward a good fight. They hunted, they killed, they feasted. And this one—

Simone whirled, bringing his axe around in an arc, using his hips to power his swing. He caught the beast mid-leap, bisecting the creature with the ease of a hot knife through lard. The two halves fell to either side of the barbarian, showering him in hot blood. Too easy.

He would die this day, but not to a feckless shit stain like a wolf. He turned in a tight circle. All around him were the glinting eyes in the shadows. A pack of wolves? Was that a worthy death?

No, he decided as the pack leapt into action. He met them with the fury of a man determined to lay waste to any and all things that might challenge him. The axe swung in a wide circle, an extension of Simone's body. He had carried the weapon for so long it was as much a part of him as his breath or his rage.

It was a frenzied blur that filled that clearing in Sarkesh. Howls and yips and agonizing whimpers floated across the air as the barbarian of Tammetta cut through the flurry of beasts. He was bored. This was no challenge, these simple things simply throwing themselves at him. Trying to catch his blind spot was the height of their cunning. It was too little. He could not go to hell unbloodied. He dropped his axe and caught the last wolf by the throat as it lunged at him. Looking into the beast's maw, Simone reached forward, grabbed the wolf's tongue, and ripped it from the root before tossing both wolf and tongue away. Too easy. Let the creature bleed out or starve. That was its punishment for attacking—

A horrifying wail split the air. Simone whirled, his hand reaching for the hilt of his axe, his rheumy eyes seeking some sign of this new threat. There was nothing in the trees, nothing in the sky. But some small movement caught his eye. One of the severed wolf legs was crawling across the ground. No—not one of them—*all* of the corpses were moving, coming together. Simone's hand tightened on his axe. He was no superstitious fool, shrieking at the undead like one of those nonces from the city might. But even his hot blood ran cold at the sight before him.

The corpses of the wolves merged together, melding into a monstrous amalgamation of claws and jaws. The patchwork monster rose from the ground, bipedal and furious. It opened its dozen maws and let loose a terrifying howl, its eyes—at least twenty of them facing Simone—burned with a vile spectral fire as it began to move forward.

This.

This was worthy death.

Simone did not question the force behind this abomination. It did not matter. The blood rage was upon him, the world awash with a red haze that sang in his ears and pounded through his skull. He threw himself at the creature, his axe screaming through the air. Each limb he separated from the creature flew through the air, only to be caught by a tether of blood that brought it right back to the beast, reattaching so it could continue the fight.

Simone did not notice. He would not have cared even if he had noticed. All that mattered was the battle. It did not matter that the blood was cursed; it only mattered that it was shed.

One of the creature's many jaws clamped tight on Simone's axe arm. The wolf head extended as though it were a fleshy tendril and whipped Simone around before releasing him. The barbarian's body soared through the crisp air and crunched into a tree. Simone felt his arm shatter. His ribs were crushed. Blood leaked through his teeth.

He slowly rose, unsteady on his feet as he raised his good arm. He couldn't speak. His lungs didn't have the air. The monster was coming at him. He couldn't roar a challenge, but he could meet it. Simone staggered forward, raising his fist for one final blow that would never land.

***

The clearing was not silent. Simone's broken body had been torn apart by the horrid amalgamation. But it was not still. He had fought hard that his soul may find its way to eternal battle in hell, but he was denied. His soul joined the wolves. His body subsumed, added to the mass of the creature that had killed him. No, he would not go to hell. But his rage lived on, his lust for violence, for blood, his hunger. Simone's roar joined the howl of the wolves, and the creature that would be known as the Tammetta Wolf stalked into the woods to find its next battle.

Calamity

(Desiree Baltisberger)

The bonfire raged in the center of the clearing, the flames leaping towards the moonless sky above. The women danced around the fire, their bodies coated in a sheen of sweat, their eyes dilated as the mushrooms took hold. Nechrubel had blessed the world with his dark administrations, and they were his wives, rutting with each other and with the demons that came forth, cursing the land, spreading forth the terror of the end in jubilant celebration. They were witches.

Desiree sat on a palanquin of bone taken from infants and drunkards. Each femur, radius, and scapula carefully removed without killing the donor. A throne of living death. She sat at the right hand of the only power that still existed in this damned world. She lorded over the death of all, swimming in the hate and violence as though it were the most soothing spring water. She watched her sisters and daughters dance around the clearing, only pausing to engage in lurid acts of sapphic desire and cannibalistic horror before those who survived rose to dance again.

The world called them *Miseries*. Such disrespect, spitting in the face of the Lord Nechrubel. Pain and terror were gifts, all that this world deserved, lovingly passed down from the cracked obsidian palace of the midnight stars to a populace that didn't deserve it. Four had come thus far, inching the world ever closed to its final ragged gasp of polluted air. It was glorious, and their fevered bacchanal here tonight would help usher in the fifth. One more day gone, one less heartbeat for the world to bear.

Torches in the distance.

Desiree saw them coming, men in their clanking armor, hiding their worthless shriveled cocks behind comically large codpieces. They rode starving horses and carried blasphemy and hate in their hearts, fed by the insecurity caused by being born a worthless wastrel of flesh in a world that cared nothing for them. Servants of the Basilisks, the slaves of Josilfa the Prude. Desiree did not react; she did not warn her sisters or order them to disband. The work was too important, and lives were too small and meaningless, to abandon it.

She didn't react when the soldiers of the Chvrch burst into the clearing, nor did she react as her sisters screamed and fled to hide behind her throne. She merely watched as the soldiers marched forward, kicking over effigies or stabbing any woman who was too caught up in lust or gluttony to have noticed the danger—skewering them, disemboweling them, and then leaving their corpses amongst the violated dead.

"By order of the Chvrch!" the head of these interlopers shouted as he approached her throne.

Desiree reached down without looking away from the captain and gripped the back of the woman's head between her thighs. "I did not tell you to stop," she whispered. The woman stared up at her in shock and fear for a moment before taking a deep breath and returning to her work. Her tongue flicked against Desiree as she lapped and sucked eagerly, forgetting the danger and trading self-preservation for pleasuring her queen and priestess.

Desiree ran her fingers through the woman's hair, adjusting her hips to give the woman better access. She found the audience helped. She reached up, running a hand over her breast, squeezing, giving the men a show. She enjoyed how the lust warred with disgust and rage in their hearts, even as their bodies responded with crude need. Needs that would never be met. Hers was the only orgasm that would matter tonight.

"By all that is holy, I command you to stop!" the captain shouted shakily, his voice trembling with his own inability to grasp a woman's sexuality on display.

"There is nothing holy here to command me," Desiree said, her voice husky as she neared climax. "But if you want me to stop, if you want me to end, then come and end me on your blade, unless you would rather finish me yourself." She brought her leg up, propping it on the arm of her throne, giving her servant even greater access and the men a better view.

"Gods damn it!" the captain growled. He knew he was losing this fight. If he let it go on, his men would abandon their faith to fuck these women. They would be devoured and their souls damned to the hells for their weakness. He marched up the path to the throne, mounted it, and drew his blade.

Desiree ignored him. Her heavy chest rose and fell as her breathing quickened. She let out a full-throated moan.

"Do it, coward," she hissed as she bucked her hips. "Penetrate me," she commanded, and he obeyed, ramming his sword through her chest, between her breasts, crushing her sternum and slicing into her heart as he pinned her to her grisly perch. He thought he was ending her. But she rode the blade through her orgasm with a maniacal laughter that turned into a hysterical scream of mirth as fire began to rain from the sky. "The sky shall weep fire, and a great stone shall plummet as a city fallen from heaven. Its gift is Death, and madness is its herald!" she cried, reaching down to hold her slave's face in place between her legs, her other hand pointing up. In the starless darkness, something loomed, growing larger every second. They would die this night, but in her sacrifice of blood and cum, the world would join her in the death throes of ecstatic agony.

Blood gushed from her mouth as she pulled herself free of the chair, pulling the sword with her, and rose, her naked form the very archetype of terrible beauty and sensuality. She was blessed by Nechrubel, she was his herald, she was the end, and now that her part was played, she would rejoin him at his side.

"Look at that, Captain," she hissed as she pulled the blade from her chest and let it fall to the ground. "You finally satisfied a woman."

He wasn't listening. His eyes stared up at the coming of death, his mind emptied and hollowed out so only madness could take hold in the seconds he had left. The night air was filled with Desiree's laughter.

Then there was a terrible crushing explosion of sound as the city of stone met the earth.

And then there was silence.

They Speak

(Nate Southard)

"I'm pretty sure you're the asshole here." Marcus Langum sighed. "Not me."

"Well, I'm pretty sure we're both assholes. So there's that," Belum shot back, his voice soft and high like a small child, despite the ragged necromancer being well into his fifties.

"Asshole or not, in this case, I'm right," Marcus said, rubbing his eyes, extremely tired of Belum's lunacy. They had traveled together for the better part of two months, and while the necromancer was skilled and could carry his weight in a fight, he had ... eccentricities that were extremely frustrating. "Our mark is in there," Marcus said, pointing into the woods. "If we want to get paid and be able to sleep indoors, we need to follow him."

"Yes," Belum agreed. "We need to get him, and he knows that, that's why he went in there. Because he knew it would be suicide to follow him."

Markus stared at the sickly man. He hated him. His stupid bald head, his ghastly stooped shoulders, his nagging persistence that all people were awful. It didn't matter that he was often right; it was still gods-damned annoying. And this? This refusal to go into the woods? It was worse. "This isn't fucking Sarkesh, Belum. It's Egin Woods. It ain't cursed." Well, it wasn't *more* cursed than any other place, anyway.

"It's the woods, you tool, they are all cursed," the necromancer snapped back.

"Be that as it may, I'm going in there to get our man. Either you come with me, or you wait out here on your own." And with that, Marcus marched down the path into the woods, cursing all the way through.

Belum stood watching for a moment, hating that his companion was so naive as to trust the wooded area. Didn't he understand the danger? No, of course he didn't. He would die in there if Belum didn't follow. After a few more moments of avoiding the inevitable, Belum ducked his head and walked resolutely into the woods. Of course, by then, he had already lost sight of Marcus. Damn the man's healthy legs and long stride. Still, Belum didn't call out for him. The less said in the woods, the less they would hear and be able to use against him in the future. He reached into his cloak and wrapped his bony fingers around an unclean scroll kept close to his heart in case of emergency.

After several minutes, Belum found Marcus. At least, what was left of Marcus. The man had been ambushed, his throat slit and his body strung between the trees as though to create a ghastly work of art. He had been disemboweled too, many of his organs littering the dirt beneath his suspended body. There was Marcus's liver laying in the dirt. Belum frowned. It was probably rude to eat a friend's organs. Was it rude to reanimate them? Sure, Langum would be a mindless undead slaved to his will, but he would be around and they could keep traveling together. Really, it would be a dick move to leave his corpse here and *not* reanimate him.

Belum suddenly whirled around, his eyes narrowed.

Reanimation after revenge. He needed to find that damned killer. He brought his scroll out, ready to unleash the corrupted power of his magic at his foe.

"You may think you have the upper hand, that I am an old man, an easy target. I assure you that the halls of my past are filled with the unquiet dead who have made that mistake," Belum hissed.

"Oh, he's terrified of you; that's for sure."

The whisper came from behind him. Belum whirled and eyed Marcus's corpse.

"Marcus?" he asked.

"Nope." The voice wasn't coming from the corpse but from the left … from the tree.

"Ah fuck! I knew it! I knew it!" Belum growled. "I knew you could talk!" Fucking trees. Shifty wooden bastards, all of them!

"Well, yes." The tree chortled. "We see, we listen, we speak."

"I'm not insane. Did you do this?" Belum accused, jabbing a dirty finger into Marcus's splayed-open chest, accidentally prodding one of his lungs.

"No, of course not. I'm a tree," the tree said smugly.

"I know you're a tree," Belum said, scowling deeply. "That's *why* I'm sure you had something to do with this." He put his hands on his waist. He shouldn't be speaking to the untrustworthy vegetation. He should be getting out of here, or at least finding the killer and *then* getting out of here. But there was one more thing bothering him. "Why *are* you speaking to me? You lot have never revealed yourselves before."

"Oh, to distract you," the tree said in a sing-song voice.

"To distra—" Belum started but was unable to finish the question, as a hand clamped down over his mouth from behind and his throat was cut deep enough to sever the chords. He collapsed. His quarry, a disgusting bandit, leaned

over him to finish sawing off his head. Somewhere deep in
the forest, the trees roared with laughter.

Kiss of the Emerald Scabies

(Lucas Baltisberger)

One more day. One more night. That's all Lucas could hope for. He stumbled through the alley and nearly collapsed against a wall. The bright-green sores along his arm itched terribly. They were infected, but he couldn't help himself. He scratched at the oozing lesions, verdigris fluid squirting and gushing down his arm as he did. It had been less than a fortnight—just a matter of days, really—and already, this terrible illness had advance so far.

A smattering of days ago, Lucas Flor had been on leave from the garrison. An upstanding member of Grift's naval forces, he acted prim and proper at all times, a stoic and often silent arbiter of the business of running an army. So on his days off, he needed to blow off steam, and what better way to do so than in one of the many brothels of Grift. In recent years, they had upped their game too. There was no act you couldn't buy, no form of companion you couldn't lease for an hour or two. The pleasure houses of Grift had thrown off the shackles of propriety's illusion.

There was one brothel that specialized in inhuman pleasures, from the spirits of slain prostitutes to inhuman sirens who fed on your lust and left you drained. But even those creatures were not the deadliest. You could pay to lay with a vampire or be penetrated by things with no human shape but so many pseudopods. Or ... if you were depraved enough, they had a supply of goblins, and you could "enjoy" yourself and then slit the creature's throat before its curse took hold.

Other brothels offered cruelty, torture, murder, drugs—any vice you could experience was for sale in Grift.

Lucas was uninterested in the vast majority of these things. He had no interest in forcing himself on any creature; he considered the act as loathsome as one could engage in. Sure, kill the fucking goblins, but don't ... torture them. Don't abuse them. He knew from experience that those people were trapped in there. Lucas felt there was enough cruelty in the world without engaging in such for sport. It was also dangerous. How many corpses were carted out of these places each day from clients who had taken chances or been careless? Served them right, as far as Lucas was concerned.

His personal vice was for the strange. Madame Coilani's House featured the strangest: survivors of arcane catastrophe. Those poor unfortunates who had been cursed or undergone terrible transformation. There was a certain exotic eroticism to their mutations. Inhuman? Maybe. But their minds and bodies were their own, and Lucas paid good coin to enjoy them. This time, though, he was suffering for it. He had found a dark-skinned woman in the back room of an opium den. She sported spots on her body that glowed with an eerie green light, like emeralds set in the dark earth. She had been breathtaking, and he hadn't hesitated to spend his entire week's salary for several hours.

It had been worth every penny. The woman was no novice and had known her way around the acts that Lucas proposed with an expertise that made him want to wed her. At the end of the night, he was spent, and so he stumbled through the streets of Grift, satiated, back to his own bed back at the garrison. When he had woken, a single painful cyst had formed on his chest. It glowed with a green luminescence that seemed much less beautiful on his leathery salt-stained skin than it had on hers.

And by god, did it itch. He had scratched and scratched, but it just made the cyst ooze, and that ooze had spread the affliction. Under the cysts, he could swear he saw the movement of some long worm-like thing. He tried to ignore that. He tried to ignore it all and continue on with his life. It hadn't worked. By the end of the first day, he could do nothing but scratch his spreading emerald growths. The painful itchiness was his entire existence. He had dragged himself to healers, to apothecaries, even to a witch, all in prayer that they could ease his suffering, cure this malady. The witch had made him disrobe and then laughed and laughed at his swollen pustule-studded cock. She had continued laughing right up until he had buried his blade in her eye socket to the hilt.

Even now, he felt like he could feel her laughter following him as he stumbled through the shadows of the alley. How much of the fluid oozing down his legs was glowing green pus, and how much was blood from ruptured sores? His head was swimming. His legs buckled and gave out. He groaned as he tried to roll onto his back, but he was too weak. All he could do was wallow in the filth of his own shed effluvia, but he could still feel. And he felt *them*.

A dozen or more rats emerged from the darkness to take timid bites of the infected man, their desperate hunger making them ignore the obviously tainted and still living nature of their meal. Lucas tried to scream, but his lungs filled with green fluid that leaked from the corner of his mouth and wept from his ears and eyes. He choked on his tongue, unable to protest as the rats devoured him and his sickness, ready in turn to spread it through the rest of Grift, a gift from Madame Coilani.

Disagreements

(Independent Legion)

"Listen to me, Alessandro." Cristiano sighed. "There are too many issues with your plan. We have to go in hard, fast. We have to surprise them.

"Rushing will only lead to our deaths," Alessandro argued. "Besides, why rush when Niccolò is still working on deciphering their missives?"

"To be fair," Niccolò said, "I've gotten through most of these missives. I think we're ready to strike if you are."

"I'm ready to strike. I want overwhelming force. I want to bring extreme violence and skill to our enemies, drown them in blood," Cristiano cried.

"I know you do; I know you do," Alessandro said, rubbing his eyes. These two would be the death of him, not that they were unskilled. Cristiano was a terribly efficient scout, searching and finding the slightest advantage to take into battle and end their foes. Niccolò, on the other hand, was no simple scribe or archivist. He had studied countless scrolls—clean, unclean, salt-crusted, and mud stained. His grasp of magic was as developed as one could attain without going mad. Alessandro's own skill came from meticulous planning and strategy. Between the three of them and a handful of mercenaries, there was no obstacle they could not overcome. But that confidence could easily turn to hubris, and hubris would see all three of them dead. That was what he was trying to curtail in his hesitance.

The three of them were gathered in a small room of a storehouse, meticulously planning the defense of their employer, the city of Eckik. In between them, lit by a number of candles, sat a table covered in maps of the city and surrounding environs. Several pages of notes, reports, and other details on the city and the invading force were laid out alongside the map, giving Alessandro an overview of the entire conflict, or at least what they *knew* of the entire conflict.

"Consider, we know their forces, we know our forces," Cristiano continued to argue. "We know the terrain; we know the weather. What don't we know? What have we to consider? And why, for the love of He and She, do we need to have some convoluted plan of attack?"

"You're overconfident," Alessandro spat, frustrated. Was he or was he not the leader of their band? "We strike when I say we strike, no sooner, no later. Do you understand me?" He had meant for it to be firm, but it came out as a snarl. The other two men looked at him with something akin to weary caution.

"Yes, Alessandro," Cristiano said softly.

"Perfectly, Lord," Niccolò muttered.

"Good," Alessandro said. "Now, the only thing we don't know is what section of the city they are targeting, nor when they will attack." He bent over the maps and papers spread over the table and scratched his chin. "That is crucial. Until we know their plan, we won't know exactly how they are spreading their force out, and until we know that, we will take greater casualties than necessary. Can you scry any of this information, Niccolò?"

***

Alessandro frowned, looking up from the maps to where Niccolò had been standing. He was gone. No sign of him at all. "Where the fuck did he go?" He snapped his eyes to Cristiano. "Where did Niccolò go?"

Cristiano frowned, he had been as focused on the papers as Alessandro had. He hadn't seen where the mage had gone. He slowly pulled a long, cruel dagger from his belt. "Something isn't right. Niccolò wouldn't just leave." He moved to where the mage had been standing, looking for any clue as to where the man had gone. Most would see nothing, but Cristiano was not most. His practiced eye caught the scuffs in the dust and grime of the floor, faint but present. Niccolò had been dragged away into the shadows.

But the shadows hid no secrets from them. There were no trap doors, no hidden mechanisms. If he had been dragged into the shadows, in the shadows he would remain. Cristiano grabbed one of the candles off the table and marched to the corner of the room. No evidence of anything, just two drag marks into the corner and then ... nothing. As though he had just disappeared.

"Something is fucked, Alessandro. We should get out of here." Cristiano turned back to the table, but Alessandro was gone. He was alone. Cristiano darted back to the table, moving around it to where Alessandro had been mere seconds ago. Two scuff marks showed that he, too, had been dragged into the shadows. Cristiano whirled around, his dagger held out before him as though to ward off whoever was coming for him.

"Alessandro! Niccolò!" he called. "This better be a goddamn trick! It is not funny!" There was ice in his stomach, an itchiness to his limbs. He just knew something was terribly wrong. A chill swept through his body. He felt rather than saw something standing behind him. He whirled in place, bringing the blade of his dagger up and punching out with it at neck height.

A cold hand gripped his wrist, and frost crept over Cristiano's flesh, his blood freezing, his skin blistering and blackening under the icy touch. The figure—a gaunt, colorless man in all black—smiled, revealing oversized canines. "Anthelia sends her greetings." The voice tolled like church bells crumbling into eternity. And without another word, he leapt into the rafters above and tore out Cristiano's throat with his teeth. There, the company of blood-thirsty dead feasted on the flesh and fluids of the three men, leaving nothing but discarded papery corpses for the city guard to find in the morning.

Dry-docked

(Brian Colin)

A single beep woke him up.

How long had he drifted in the void between stars? Ensign Brian Colin of the *Blind Mariah* couldn't remember. He could, of course, check any of the instruments that blinked across the mostly empty deck. They would tell him in excruciating detail how long he had been meandering through space. How long it had been since he had been forced to fight for his life. How long it had been since he had been confronted by the inevitability of the Grimm.

But he didn't want to know.

It would only add to the weight of his despair. He had served aboard the *Mariah* for a few short years, a contract engineer and gunner working contracts with a crew trying to make a few bucks before trying to find some way to escape the end of the universe. They had been so optimistic that he had believed them. He had adopted their familial demeanor, their hope contagious. But this last job ...

It had felt like any other job, an easy one, even. No hiccups, no problems, no red flags. It wasn't until Belinda had begun complaining about headaches that anyone had an inkling that something had not gone perfectly. It wasn't until she had shown up with her eyes glowing blue and her veins bright pink that they had realized *what* had gone wrong. And by then, it was too late.

Brian didn't know how long the siege of the bridge had gone on, for the same reason he didn't know how long it had been since. He didn't want to know how long it had taken for every one of his friends to become one of the Grimm, how long it had taken him to kill them all. One shotgun blast at a time, he had dealt death to death as it came knocking. He did keep count, of course. He knew every member of the crew, and he counted down as they died until the countdown reached one. Him. He was alone. He had locked the flight deck down, and then, in a fit of terror, he had opened every door on the ship to the void, allowing near explosive decompression to rip the remains of his adopted family and every damned worm they had brewing in their skulls to the emptiness of the void.

He had slept on and off since then, eating what prepackaged food was stowed in the claustrophobic room, the crushing silence of eternity his only companion. Until now.

Brian pulled himself to the console and looked over the instruments and screens, trying to figure out what exactly was calling for attention. It might be the life support. He might be running out of air. He didn't want that. He was even more terrified of death than he was of the Grimm. It was why he was still alive. His shotgun had one more shell, and he had secured his safety before venting the ship. But it wasn't the life support. It was a proximity alarm.

Gasping, Brian opened the shutters, revealing the outside world to him for the first time in … he had no idea how long. The stars were revealed slowly as the tempered titanium slowly rolled back from the specially treated glass to reveal a space station looming dead ahead. Joy filled Brian's heart. He was saved. He could get off the ship and … and why weren't they hailing him? Brian reached out and flipped the comms switch on and off and on again. Static filled the ship, and then ... a sound.

It was almost unnoticeable, background noise against the static of an unmanned radio. But it was unmistakable. It was the eldritch groan of the Grimm. The hated whisper of a thousand worm-filled mouths chanting the prophecies of dead stars. It was madness. It was terror. It was welcoming him home.

Brian stared ahead. He could steer clear—hell, if left to its own devices, the ship's autopilot would do that on its own. He would survive for another day, maybe another week in his little space-faring hovel ... That is what he *should* do. But this was an entire space station of Grimm, an entire populace infected, ready to spread across the stars and strip away more families, murder more hope.

Brian no longer feared death in that moment. He reached across the consoles, quickly typing, quickly rerouting power and changing parameters, dismissing warnings and klaxons as they began to sound. He turned off the ship's autopilot and gritted his teeth as he grabbed the steering column and set course for the heart of the space station, where its own reactor would be quietly humming away. This was no heroic end. It wouldn't save the universe. It wouldn't even make a dent. But it *was* revenge. It was the last bit of control a desperate man had.

"For Belinda," Brian whispered as he steered the *Mariah* into a thunderous collision with the space station just as the *Mariah's* reactor went critical. There was no pain—there was no time. There was only the sudden blinding light of one man's determination to end things on his own terms.

The Portrait of Madness

(Nohr)

ohr stared bleary-eyed at the portrait in front of him. It was the 72nd attempt at painting Lord Figas. He wanted to paint something that would honor the count, something that would please him. Or more accurately, he wanted to be *finished* with it. He wanted to be paid and left to spend his coin at the nearest tavern on whatever mediocre meat they had smoked, whatever mediocre mead they had fermented, and whatever mediocre whore they employed for a mediocre evening. It was all anyone could hope for this is SHE-forsaken land.

He had meant to paint the count in the most flattering light possible. Focusing on the brightness of his clothes, the clear blue of his eyes, and the fullness of his beard. By all the gods in hell, he had fully intended to. But every time he sat staring at the count's hated visage, he ended up highlighting his syphilis sores and herpes-laden lips. No, not highlighting, that would imply that they were somehow *more* subtle under the count's boorish makeup. But the caked-on greasepaint only served to amplify the oozing puss and unnatural pallor around each puckered abscess.

Nohr frowned at the splattering of yellow and black paint. It was an abstraction of the count. A caricature of jagged lines and dynamic splotches that elevated his sickly countenance to something monstrous. No, not elevated. Nohr's portrait was perfectly accurate. It matched the man's soul, if a man such as that could be said to have a thing as banal as a soul.

"Well, boy?" The count's voice was a warbling bellow. The shouting of a child who had never been told no, not once in his horrid life, and so had never learned to temper his demands with reason. "How goes *this* painting? Perhaps you feel comfortable enough to cease hiding your vision? Mmmh? You came very highly recommended from the Duchess of Verikhonne. I want to see what all her fuss was about."

Nohr offered a flitting smile, an expression that scampered across his face like a rat startled by a loud noise. He would have to remember to thank Giselda for the recommendation. He was sure she was trying to help him, trying to reward him for his dedication to both art and pleasuring her while her boorish husband was with one of his whores, but still ... This was less a reward and more of a strange hell that he had been thrust into.

He knew that showing any of the paintings to the count would lead to him being thrown out, possibly a few broken bones. But on the other hand, hadn't he slaved away enough for these blue-blooded fucks? He'd had broken hands before; he had been thrown out of places in the past. He didn't need the money that badly.

Fuck it. "Yes, Lord," Nohr finally responded. "Very good, I think it's a perfectly accurate portrayal of His Lordship." He reached up and grabbed the top edge of the canvas, lifting it from the easel and turning it to face the count. He held the painting over his face so he could hide his somewhat deranged grin. Better or worse, this terrible assignment was over.

Nohr had expected to hear shouting, or accusations,

something. After what felt like several moments, he lowered the canvas, resting the bottom of the artwork on his boot as he met the count's eyes.

He wished he hadn't.

The man was smiling. His teeth, blackened and rotting in his mouth, made Nohr wince as the clicked together. "Ah, you truly do have an eye, don't you? Very visionary, very … astute." The words slid out of the corpulent bastard. "This is what you see when you look at me?" he asked.

Nohr fumbled over the words. It was one thing to snub a noble; it was another to insult them to their face. "I … have a bit of a style. It isn't to everyone's taste," he finally managed to spit out.

"No. Not to everyone's taste. Speaking of taste." He waved his hand.

Suddenly, hands grabbed Nohr from behind, pinning his arms to his side. He fought against them but was held fast.

"Let me go!" Nohr growled, squirming and kicking out, but to no avail. The count's guards were stronger than he was. Their gauntlets dug into his flesh painfully. The count pushed himself out of his chair, his bulk jiggling as he found his balance, then he approached the bound artist.

"Your vision? Remarkable. Your taste, unique. I would have both." He reached to Nohr's face, his thumbs slipping into his skull to hook behind the orbs, and, slowly, almost lovingly, pulled both eyes from their sockets. Nohr's vision swung around wildly as his eyes fell free, dangling from the optic nerves. He watched, screaming, as the count lifted the right eye and bit into it, his vision in that eye going dark as he watched teeth descend into the meat. The orb popped between the count's teeth, ocular jelly spilling over his jowls.

"Exquisite," he moaned before repeating the process with Nohr's left eye.

Nohr continued to scream, but it was a hoarse whisper

of nothing against the laughter of the guards and the noisy slurping of the count.

"Delicious and decadent, you have earned your reward." The voice sounded so far away. Nohr begged for mercy, for death, for anything other than this current reality. "Nonsense, you worked so hard, my dear artist, and for that, you must be paid. Better than gold, better than jewels or any currency there is." The count cupped Nohr's cheek for a moment before leaning forward to shove his tongue in the empty eye socket and slurp up some of the loose juices within.

"Ah, take him." He gestured and turned his back. The count listened as Nohr was dragged away, his terrified shrieks filling the castle. Some would say the count was cruel or evil, but they were deluded, all of them. How could he explain how kind he truly was? Being allowed to work for the count, to paint him? The painting would be displayed next to Nohr's still writhing body as he was strung up outside the castle and eaten away by the elements and scavengers. All would see him; all would know him.

After all, what better payment was there than exposure?

Method of Death

1) Monster

2) Trap

3) Disease

4) Scvm

5) Accident

6) Curse

7) Arcane Catastrophe

8) Roll Twice and Combine

Monster

1) HeartBats

Your lust for silver has once again brought you to yet another dark and muggy cavern. The echoing skitters of hidden creatures never bothered you, so with your guard down, you stumble across a nest of HeartBats among countless corpses. Before you can react, your chest is pierced by one of these flying terrors, their proboscis pumping egg after egg into your beating heart. You know in less than a week, these eggs will hatch and burst from your torso, and there's nothing you can do about it.

2) Hoarder Orb (from Book of Bitter Biles)

An old man in the last tavern you were in hands you a map to an old keep just outside town, asking you to recover a small music box that used to belong to his daughter. When the right amount of silver is mentioned, you make your way there to find the rooms and halls cleared out of everything and the floors have not a speck of dust. Opening the last room on the far end of the keep reveals a monstrosity of slime and home goods ... and the music box you've been sent to retrieve. After a long, hard-fought battle, you're bested by the slime as a tentacle shoots into your mouth and down your throat, suffocating you where you stand. All the while, the music box plays ... slowing as your heart does the same ... matching tempo until they both stop.

3) Zukuma (Core book)

Night terrors have plagued your sleep for longer than you can remember. The visions of your village brutally slain by berserkers stand in the way of a good night's rest. You wander the dying lands with no purpose or direction ... until the horns that echo through your dreams howl in the distance. Running isn't an option ... you've already been spotted. A band of Zukuma crest a distant hill, sprinting towards you, chain swords and war mauls in hand. The screams that haunt your slumber are the last you hear.

4) The Windspirit (from Bestiary)

The search party has been at it for six straight days ... "Where can these damn kids be?" Not that you care. You're only in this for the reward. Deep into the night, you lose sight of the rest of the party ... I'm sure the pulls off your flask didn't help matters... So in an attempt to not get yourself more lost, you lay in the grass and stare at the sky with a head full of spirits. As the clouds shift, threatening to burst into a storm, you hear what sounds like whispers in the distance ... "Come, my child ... You are hungry, and I will lead you to eat ..." Are the assholes from the search party fucking with you? Did those little shits finally show up? "Come, my child ... You are hungry, and I will lead you to eat ..." Ringing louder now ... ominously echoing in your mind ... echoing so much that you fail to realize your stomach is in knots with starvation. As the voices subside, the urge to feed grows to the point that you're foaming at the mouth and your whole body shakes with ravenous anticipation. "Paul, where did your drunk ass go?" Hearing the party walking your way puts you in a rage, and as you charge the group, you are shot down dead in your tracks by a crossbow bolt. The last thing you hear echoing in your head as your life slips away is "Come, my child ... You are hungry, and I will lead you to eat ..."

5) Ragpie (Bergen Chrypt, from Feretory)

Sorting through the discarded clothing at the crematorium for loose silver has been the only thing that has kept your opium addiction at bay. As you approach the next pile of tattered attire, you notice a pile of freshly gnawed on bones, flesh ripped violently from them. As you kneel down to investigate the horrific scene, the pile of clothes burst towards you in a flurry of talons, beaks, and feathers. Petrified by the site, the wings completely envelope you as this demon bird continues clawing and pecking at your flesh. In no time, you are reduced to a pile of fleshless bones. Was that fix worth it?

6) Gawking Harpy (from Tales & Poetry of Sarkash)

You've taken your father's place, transporting goods from Ichorthorn, on the edge of Sarkash, to the once great city of Galgenbeck. The only words of warning from the withered old man were to "Watch the tree line for haunting eyes ..." Disregarding the old fool's advice, you venture off on your maiden voyage. As day turns to night, the road becomes dark and ominous, and bedding down for the night seems like a good idea. As you set up camp, an eerie silence suddenly takes over the area. In the distance, you think you spot the reflection of your campfire off two tiny globes, but the moment you move to investigate, they disappear ... then reappear in the complete opposite direction. As the night presses on, the advice your father gave you races through your head. Losing the fight with exhaustion of the travel day and your overactive imagination, you begin to fade into slumber. Just as you do, you wake to see winged creatures surrounding you. The moment you reach for your crossbow, the creatures shriek in unison and shred your flesh from head to toe and feast on your corpse.

Trap

1) In the search for some rumored silver in a long-forgotten coal mine, you trip on a rusted wire, triggering the roof to collapse and bury you and your party under tons of rubble, never to be heard from again.

2) Lost in the forest of Sarkash for d6 days in search of food, you hear the whimpers of an injured rabbit. Furiously sprinting towards your next meal, you overlook the poorly covered pit with crude spikes stuck in the bottom, impaling you next to the rabbit you were seeking.

3) A faint glow piques your curiosity from across the long corridor. Traversing the hall shows a glyph that seems to beckon you closer, almost overlooking the piles of bone and innards at the foot of it. Touching the glyph instantly liquifies your skin and adds your corpse to the pile you were just standing in.

4) You travel north through the frigid lands of Allians, hoping to escape the immeasurable gambling debt you've collected from the Arch-Rogue of Schleswig, when you lose your balance on the slick icy road. Reaching for the closest tree only rattles loose a hail storm of icy needles, shredding your flesh from bone. Little do you know that the Arch-Rogue knew your escape plans and sent goons to come collect.

5) A lone statue of Fathmu IX stands stoic in the courtyard you frequently visit, mocking you since his lackeys took your gong farm. Drunk and enraged one stormy night, you decide to dismantle the grotesque carving, only to be petrified alive by the cursed statue, suffocating in your stone-skinned tomb.

6) Out on a hunting excursion in the SvmpLands, looking for Frogmen to feed your village, you trip on some unseen roots in the marsh and land face first in a bubble of Acidic gas, melting your face to the bone and alerting the Frogmen to finish the job.

Disease

1) Pox

You were once a respected member of the village council, stern but fair. When the old crone from the outskirts of town came to ask for an extension on her taxes, you declined, stating everyone needs to pay their fair share. Enraged by your decision, the crone muttered a few indecipherable words and spit in your face. You wake in the middle of the night with your bedding and nightgown stuck to you and your newly open weeping sores. The next morning, you are immediately relieved of your duties on the council and forced to leave town, as to not spread your newfound ailment. The only one to say goodbye is the crone you jilted the day before.

2) Leprosy

Who knew a small nip would cause such a huge problem?! The opossum living in the church's rafters has a bad attitude and a worse bite! As the days go by, the flesh rots and falls from bone. Within a week, any semblance of skin and muscle is long gone ... and there's no sign of it stopping at your limb.

3) Brainworms

NEVER TRUST A TRAVELLING BUTCHER! You've been told this your entire life, but the deal on pork was too good to pass up! With a belly full of ham slabs and chops, your stomach starts to turn and your flesh crawls as you see what could only be described as worms traveling just under the surface of your skin upwards to your head. Paralyzed in fear, you let it happen as the worms burrow into your brain. The excruciating headache that follows is your second concern. Your first? Your insatiable craving for flesh.

4) Crimson Decay

Deep in the catacombs of a long-forgotten tomb, you and your party are lost and are funneled into a narrow hallway. As you all squeeze through, you are aided by a sweet-smelling red ooze, covering the walls. Not thinking anything of it, you and your party press on, looking for an exit. What feels like days later, you finally reach the surface, only to have that sweet-smelling red ooze react to the light drizzle of rain and start to burn through your clothing ... and flesh ...

5) Hydrophobia:

Four long fruitless days on a hunting trip have worn on you ... Good thing you have your trusted hound, Grundle, with you. As the sun sets in the west, you and your companion are ambushed by a pack of wolves, frothing at the mouth. Trying your best to fend them off, you both are bitten several times. You rush to the river to clean your wounds before they set, and the mere sight of the rushing water strikes fear into you and the dog's heart. As the days pass, even the thought of hydrating sickens the both of you ... leaving you both husks of your former selves ...

6) Slippery Sickness

Your skin constantly oozes a greasy fluid. Without shoes, you're liable to trip. Without gloves, you're liable to drop objects. The upside is that monsters will have a hard time grabbing your skin. Your days as the royal taste tester have done you well. It's an easy gig! All the food is prepared in-house daily by a trusted staff, so there's no worry of poison. You've grown rotund in this position, and happy ... Well, as happy as you can be in the paranoid court of King Sigfúm the Kind. As the days draw near to the mass egress off the cliff Terion, you have more pressing concerns ... like the thick, greasy fluid leaking from your pores, preventing you from grasping anything or keeping your balance as you slip and slide down the thirteen flights of stairs, only to be stopped by the royal guards as you bowl them down.

Human Scum:

1) *King Buzz-O, Cult Leader/Beekeeper: Bees!*

"Praise the Pollinators!" This phrase has been carved into your mind since birth ... or ever since the local beekeeper, Vatan Nifgan, started making his hallucinogenic (and deadly addictive) honey from bees he procured from a travelling salesman. Vatan, going by the title King Buzz-O these days, has been feeding the honey to the village for years, keeping them under his thrall. Your duty in the whole scheme of things is to remove the larvae from the hive boxes and place them in new ones, knowing the adult bees will devour the young. Not the easiest of jobs, but one given to a member of "The King's Court" who shows the most promise ... whatever that will get you. As you transfer larvae one morning, when the bees are most docile, you see one of the largest bees in your life feasting on the young ones. Like, a rat-sized bee! And it is wrecking the most fruitful honeycomb. As you reach for something to pry it away from the already devastated honeycomb, it turns its attention to you, grabbing your arm with its strong mandibles and sinking its stinger into your hand before ripping off its abdomen and spilling its vital organs all over you. Distracted by the pain, you fail to see the whole colony rise up and completely encompass you, biting and stinging you to death. As your attempt to take your last breath, King Buzz-O stands above you with the rest of the village, chanting, "Praise the Pollinators!"

2) *Fisk Baskins, Cannibal Cook: cook's apprentice/ground up in meat grinder*

Not the most glamorous of jobs, but it's a paycheck. You've travelled with Fisk on his food cart throughout the dying lands for only a few weeks now, but he has taken a liking to you. Your job in this team is to scour the alleys at night for whatever discarded food and vermin you can so Fisk can turn it into something edible. You're not sure how he does this, but somehow, he makes this trash into quite the tasty meal. One night, you come back to the cart early and empty handed, as the streetcleaners must have been through before you got there, only to see Fisk roasting an elderly man, still alive, with an onion shoved in his mouth to choke the screams. You scream in horror and startle Fisk as he's preparing tomorrow's special. With the quickness of a scared deer, Fisk snatches you by your neck and knocks you out with the hilt of his cleaver. You wake to being tied up and extreme pain coming from your feet. It turns out he has cut all your toes off and is eating them like candies. He instantly grabs you and shoves you feet-first into his meat grinder and slowly cranks the handle. You pass out several times from the shock of the situation, but he quickly wakes you to see the anguish and pained look on your face as he grinds your body into a pile of minced meat.

3) *Zizek Plagesopp, Arch-Rogue of the Schleswig Underground: mafia hit*

This is it, your big break ... your first job for the Arch-Rogue! A huge jump from being a lowly pickpocket scraping to make ends meet. You're in the big time now! Too bad you have to be chaperoned around by his Half-Goblin nephew, Tommy ... Either way, it's a reason to celebrate! "Drinks are on me!" you scream as you get properly tanked the night before your first gig. As the night presses on and the drinks keep flowing, Tommy reminds you that you need to keep a level of professionalism, especially right before a gig. You, completely hammered by this point, push him off and tell him to mind his business. Before you know it, you are being woken up by the waters of a freezing river, head screaming with the worst hangover you've ever had. The first thing you see is Tommy's face, jagged grin and all, as he proceeds to hold your head under that frigid water. As the last breath escapes your lungs and your eyes start to fade, you see Tommy mouth the words, "This is my business ..."

4) General Cedric Balthazar, The Betrayed Phantom: haunted

In a past life, you were a respected Captain in Fathmu's militia. You led justly and followed orders explicitly, a cog in the military machine. This got the attention of one of the most feared and reviled leaders of this time, General Cedric Balthazar. Impressed by how you handle your company of men, he took you under his wing to mold you in his likeness. Cruel and heartless to soldiers and enemy alike, Balthazar only sought out blood. No justice, no humanity, just to layer the fields in bodies ... victory by any means necessary. Disgusted by his actions, you sneak into his tent one night, after a session of heavy wine drinking, and slit his throat. Just as the knife clears the neck, two guards enter the tent and see the heinous (but just) act and apprehend you. You are tried for murder but somehow spared the death penalty and sentenced to life in prison. After months of imprisonment, you start to hear whispers in your head ... Low at first, but familiar. Soon, the whispers turn into howls, then scream ... "It can't be him ... He's—he's dead! I made sure of this!" you say to yourself, and a figure appears in the corner of the room. The figure is none other than General Cedric Balthazar. "Boy, you and me are gonna be in here for a long time ..." the ghostly figure says in a gruff half-chuckle.

5) *Toddward Ingred, the Destitute Thespian: understudy*

The theatre has always been your dream. Performing is in your blood! The light, the makeup, the audience ... you crave the life (and the attention). Your drive for the arts has caught the eye of local theatre legend, Toddward Ingred. For all his talents, his reputation precedes him ... drunk... womanizer ... ash addict (how did he even get that?). But his talents are second to none. Toddward proclaims you his new understudy, which means you are his errand boy. One afternoon, after procuring Toddward's contractually binding rider (a bottle of grain alcohol, a milk maid with the glimmer of hope in her eye, and a loaf of day-old bread), you find yourself on stage with the latest script, casually reading the lines out loud. Unbeknownst to you, both the director and Toddward are there to witness you flawlessly reciting the lines—the director in the seats and Toddward by the curtain rigging. As you finish the scene, the director slow-claps from the back of the room, saying that even the great Toddward Ingred couldn't have delivered the lines better. Toddward, seeing red after hearing this absolute hogwash, starts to pull all the rigging pins for the curtains, dropping sandbag after sandbag until one drops directly onto your head, crushing you where you stand. "The Great Toddward Ingred will not be outshined!"

6) Wemut, the Catacomb Saint: sacrifice

You've made your living as a tomb raider for longer than you care to remember. And the lifestyle has been very favorable. So much so, you've taken jobs from high-ranking and wealthy individuals to find some of the rarest artifacts the dying lands have to offer. Your latest job is no exception. You've been tasked to find a set of beads called Saint Karl's Chaplet of Everlasting Life. Legend has it that breaking the beads when you are near death will revitalize you. Always up for a challenge (and silver), you make your way to the catacomb where the beads were last known to be and start exploring. Tomb after tomb, corpse after desiccated corpse ... nothing. You find yourself at the last sarcophagus, with the name Wemut carved into the lid, when you hear a shifting coming from inside. Not the first rat or scarab you've dealt with, so you pay the noise no mind. Sliding the lid over reveals the very treasure you have been searching for ... wrapped around the waist of a skeleton with surprisingly well-preserved eyes. As you reach for your prize, one of the skeletal hands grabs you and the other stabs you with a dagger that before this was hidden. As you wrestle to free yourself, the blood loss grows to be too much to deal with, and you pass out, only to be awakened by the skeleton cutting you from chest to waist, pulling your lower organs out, and dropping the beads into the cavity. The skeleton cackles, "Have fun with these, jackass!" as it slides the lid back in place, leaving you with your ill-gotten bounty to rot.

Accident:

1) Stabbed with your own dagger:

Once again, you've been "asked" by Drosten, the local blacksmith, to take a shipment of weapons to the guards at the furthest outpost, located at the summit of Mt. Prüs. You hate this trip ... The road has been washed out for years, and the trails have been overgrown with dense, thorny shrubs. Midway into your trip, you're caught in a heavy downpour, washing out the rest of the road. Determined to get this task over with, you power through, only to be caught in a landslide of rock and mud, which takes you and your cart off the road and into the thicket of thorned bushes. In your tumble, your dull dagger, the only personal weapon you own, becomes unsheathed and somehow pierces your heart, leaving you to bleed out and die in the washed-out mess of mud, thorns, and cart debris.

2) Kicked in the skull by a horse:

You have always dreamed of something greater ... something more fulfilling ... But being the only son of the town's horse farrier has you on a very different (and depressing) path. As you trim the hooves of Oslafa, the town magistrate's prize horse, preparing it for new shoes, you daydream of a future you will never have ... riches, fame, glory, a better life ... When suddenly, you're brought back to reality as the beast rears back and plants the hoof you're working on right between your eyes, splitting your skull like an overripe melon. Your father warned you that your daydreaming would get you hurt ... Father knows best.

3) Crushed by a tree:

The new recruits always seem to get the shit jobs: dig the latrine, clear the campsite of rock and debris, bury the latrine … This time, you're told to collect firewood for the camp. Not the worst job you've been assigned, so you set out with a rusty axe and 30 minutes of daylight to collect kindling. As dusk rapidly approaches, you find a rotten shell of a tree. "This should work," you think to yourself, and you start to chop at the base, not realizing there is an owl's nest 20 feet above you. As you hack away, the owl swoops down and lashes at you with its talons in an attempt to prevent you from destroying its home. Distracted by the angered bird, you don't realize that the tree you've been working on is quickly collapsing, and it comes crashing on top of you, crushing your body as the owl scratches and pecks at your eyes and face. Latrine duty doesn't seem so bad now …

4) Ran over by your own cart (changing a wheel):

Just your luck … The front wheel on your cart hit a rock and snapped in two in the middle of the worst rainstorm in known history. Luckily, as this isn't the first time you've had this happen, you have a spare. As you wrestle to get the spare on so you can get back on the road, an enormous crash of lightning erupts and startles your horse. The spooked beast decides to take off in a mad dash for safety, and the cart runs you over, crushing your chest with the rear wheel.

5) Falling down an endless pit:

The unforgiving plains of Wästland have never treated you

well ... especially after your exile from Schleswig for cheating at dice ... As you roam the vast nothingness ahead of you, you spook a sounder of Bautoboar ... and they are out to finish what the guards in the city started. Recklessly sprinting for your pathetic life, you trip and fall into a hole, a hole that doesn't seem to have a bottom ... Minutes, hours, days pass without hitting bottom ... Eventually, dehydration and starvation take you to the afterlife, with no one knowing you are missing.

6) Papercut:

"Stamp this, file that ... Is this what my life has come to?" you mutter to yourself as stacks of paperwork clutter your workspace. Distracted by dreams of a better life you feel you deserve, you mindlessly cut your hand with one of the letters you are stuffing into envelopes. Your attempts to stop the bleeding are futile as the blood keeps pumping out like it's trying to escape your body. Within minutes, you are completely exsanguinated and drop to the floor, a husk of your former self.

Curse:

1) Unstable Weight:

Your health has always been your main focus. As you see the world dying around you, you have convinced yourself that staying healthy will be vital to your survival. You eat right, properly exercise, and stay away from the indulgences in life. This has made you look down on folks who don't have the same health goals as you ... especially the barmaid you harass relentlessly. One particular evening, you order the same stew you always do, but for some reason, today's stew is especially delicious. You almost can't stop yourself from ordering bowl after bowl, to the point where you feel your clothing tightening and your stomach aching from overeating ... But you can't stop ... You won't stop! All the while, the barmaid serves you bowl after bowl of this stew, watching you gorge yourself. Eventually, the shear mass you have accumulated is too much for the chair you are in, and it splinters under your weight. The moment you try to pick yourself up, your bones crack and break. There's nothing you can do! You are stuck in the middle of the tavern, a mass of grotesque immobile flesh. As the barmaid slides a pouch of silver to a random patron, thanking them for their help, she raises a mug to the air, looking directly at you, and says, "To your health!"

2) Bad Luck:

Luck has never been on your side. As if some sort of otherworldly force is keeping you from succeeding in this world. And it's been this way for as long as you can remember. Whether it be in business, relationships, or even the simplest social interactions, the worst possible scenario always happens ... so much so, you are convinced that it is spreading... like an aura around you... that folks who come in contact with you are affected by this cloud of bad luck. And the village has suffered for your curse. Dead crops and livestock, failed businesses ... hell, even the well has dried up, so no fresh water. The worst part, they know it's you! Frustrated and at their wits end, the village has decided to take action and string you up. As they hoist you at the gallows, the rope snaps and drops you hard to the ground, breaking both your legs and your neck. But somehow, you're still alive. Disgusted by the events, the villagers leave you where you lie ... to die with the bad luck cloud you are encompassed in.

3) Whispered Madness:

Knowledge is power, or so you've been told. Your quest for knowledge has led you to an apprenticeship under the tutelage of a reclusive sage in the middle of a dead grove outside of Sarkash. He opened his library to you with the strict instructions to leave one particular tome alone. "Under NO circumstances are you to open this book! Do you understand me?" he firmly tells you. You reluctantly agree, knowing full well the first moment you get, you are going to do the thing you swore not to. One morning, the old man says he's headed to town for supplies, and you offer to stay back to tend to the meal cooking over the fire. The moment he has left your line of sight, you grab the forbidden book, open the leather straps keeping it closed, and start reading. Anticlimactically, the only thing in the book is names and dates ... absolutely no information whatsoever. You thumb through it for a few minutes, then close it and place it back on the shelf. Not more than an hour later, your head gets light and starts to spin ... The names and dates in the book start racing through your head ... Then the voices ... so many voices ... Voices of people you've never met before tell you the old man will betray you ... like he has betrayed them ... that you need to kill him to free them from the tome they are trapped in ... And as the voices become the only thing you can focus on, crippling you where you sit, the old man returns, knowing what you've done. Without hesitation, he clubs you with the back of his staff. As the voices start to fade from your mind and the blood pools on the ground, the old man grabs for the book and his quill. He opens it and looks at you. "Kratar, right? Now, what day is it again?" as he adds your name to the tome.

4) Ashen Feast:

You've traveled countless days through terrible conditions and run out of food. Poor planning on your part. In the distance, you see a small cottage with smoke billowing from a chimney. As you get closer, the smell of cooked meats takes you over. Before you could knock on the door, a frail woman opens it and beckons you in. You beg her to share her meal, and she reluctantly agrees, stating there's not much to begin with. With no regards to manners, you tear through the three rabbits she has prepared, leaving no flesh on the bones, and demand more. Disgusted and visibly angered, she prepares the last rabbit she was saving for another day. Your impatience grows by the minute until she plates the last of her food and slides it across the table. Mindlessly devouring the meal, your stomach starts to turn and you start to vomit.

But not half chewed food or bile but ash ... endless amounts of ash ... Your body can't purge the ash quick enough as you choke on the ash stuck to the back of your throat, dropping dead where you sit.

5) Vanishing Coinage:

Whenever the cursed handle currency, there's a chance a portion vanishes, making trade and purchases frustrating. Your days as a bank teller have been less than exciting. Silver coin after silver coin that passes through your hands has no meaning anymore. "What will it matter when the end comes?" you say to yourself, until one day, a young woman in finely crafted clothing comes to your booth with something you've never seen before ... a single gold coin. The shine is something unlike anything you've ever witnessed. Your greed takes over, and you pocket it rather than put it in the vault. Going about your day, your thoughts go back to that coin, and you fail to realize that every silver you touch corrodes in the bank bags. At the end of your shift, when the banker checks your ledger, they find nothing but corroded shaving in the bag and call for the authorities. Theft is poorly looked upon in this town, and you are locked in the stockade to rot for the town to watch. As you slowly die, the young woman returns, takes her gold coin back, and walks away.

6) Beast Bane:

Your days working at the royal kennels have their ups and downs. Some days, the dogs are fine, even sociable. Other days, they are downright vicious. On one of the better days, you are asked to walk the duke's finest pug, nicknamed Beans for obvious reasons, to the vet. When the dog stops and pees on the tattered robes of an old woman, you completely disregard the actions of the dog and carry on with your task as she screams nonsensical gibberish across the courtyard at you. After the visit, Beans seems more agitated than usual, growing more defiant and unruly the longer they're in your presence. Unfazed by the dog's demeanor, you take them back to the kennel and go about your day. As the next day approaches, all the dogs in the kennel are aggravated when you walk in, to the point where they are rattling their cages and lunging at you. One of the hunting mastiffs breaks free of the cage and jumps directly on you, chomping and biting at your neck. The rest of the dogs break free of their enclosures and join in on the carnage, leaving you a bloody pile of chewed flesh.

Magic Mishap: Arcane Catastrophes

17: You're staring down the elk you've been following for days to put food on the table. You've tried everything to take it down. Traps, snares, crossbow bolts ... nothing has worked. Your last chance to feed the tribe is to read the scroll you have packed away and pray it works. As you read the words off the parchment, titled Enochian Syntax, something feels ... off ... The scroll crumbles to tendrils of a fine black powder ... reaching for your mouth and nose ... clogging your airways from any chance of breathing.

13: Ale after ale fills your belly as you drown your sorrows. A Rat Catcher ... that's what you've lowered yourself to after being ousted from King Fathmu's personal guard. "Make one festering boil joke and they give ya the boot!" you mutter to yourself as a rat scampers across the bar. You slur the words of a telekinesis scroll to drop an empty mug on the rodent but miss and smash its tail. The loud squeak is followed by a quick bite. The rush of adrenaline is too much for your intoxicated situation and you pass out. You wake in what looks to be a woven wire basket, feeling ... different ... An enormous, oddly shaped man stands on the other side of the enclosure, with a whisker-like mustache. As he picks up the cage and heads towards a water-filled barrel, the last thing you hear is, "This is for my tail, varmint!"

16: The altitude has you gasping for breath as you are fighting off a pack of wolves, trying to rescue the town leader's son who they abducted. Outnumbered and desperate to collect the child (and reward), you recite the incantation on the scroll, Foul Psychopomy, to bolster your numbers. SUCCESS! Four skeletons rise from the pile of bones surrounding the wolf's den and take to arms (femurs, but beggars can't be choosers), and they charge! Problem is, they head straight for you, bludgeoning you to death as the wolves rip flesh from bone.

10: This is it! Your first adventure! Those years as an apprentice locksmith and trapper finally paid off! You study and practice using the Hermetic Step scroll you "found" in the old man's satchel in the tavern, in hopes to get rich quick! Leading the crew into the Arachno-Queen's lair should have been easy, but you stutter your words and all the torches go out ... and won't relight ... The last thing you feel is the fangs of some large spider plunge into your skull, and you hear your "party" run screaming for their lives.

7: There's no need to show off at the brothel; everyone knows their roles ... But you HAD to show your "date" your new toy ... As soon as you say the last words on the "invisibility" scroll you picked up at the market, your body becomes white hot as your skin melts off the muscle, your flesh chars from the bone, and your guts explode in an infernal hot mess on your "date."

9: As you lazily lounge in your tiny boat on Lake Onda with a head full of psychedelic fungi, you flip through an old journal handed down to you from your grandfather on his death bed with the specific direction to NOT read it. As you disregard his wishes, you see the sky warp and the stars spin ... slowly at first but quickening to the point that you vomit profusely into your boat and pass out ... Only to wake up to witness 7:7 with your own two eyes. PRAISE YETSABU-NECH!

www.ingramcontent.com/pod-product-compliance
Lightning Source LLC
Chambersburg PA
CBHW020734310726
48969CB00003B/828